'You're marri

He heard Maggie's
the sound of the wa

'N...no.'

'You wear a wedding ring.'

'So I do.'

'Why?'

'That, Dev Macafferty,' she said softly, 'is none
of your business.'

Trisha David is a country girl, born on a south-east Australian dairy farm. She moved on—mostly because the cows just weren't interested in her stories! Married to a 'very special doctor', Trisha writes Medical Romances™ as Marion Lennox and Enchanted™ stories as Trisha David. In her other life she cares for kids, cats, dogs, chooks and goldfish, she travels, she fights her rampant garden (she's losing) and her house dust (she's lost!)—oh, and she teaches statistics and computing to undergraduates at her local university.

Recent titles by the same author:

BRIDE 2000
MARRYING WILLIAM

MARRIAGE
FOR MAGGIE

BY
TRISHA DAVID

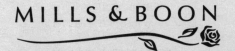

MILLS & BOON

With thanks to Julie and Sandy Cameron, proprietors
of Meredith Dairy (makers of the World's Best Goat Cheese!)
and their wonderfully helpful staff, Mary Dick and Sue Charlson.

This book is dedicated to Molly and Myrtle—
it's readers like you who make writing a pleasure!

*First published in Great Britain 1999
Harlequin Mills & Boon Limited,
Eton House, 18-24 Paradise Road, Richmond, Surrey TW9 1SR*

© Trisha David 1999

ISBN 0 263 81909 4

*Set in Times Roman 10½ on 11¾ pt.
02-0001-50944 C1*

*Printed and bound in Spain
by Litografia Rosés, S.A., Barcelona*

CHAPTER ONE

ERNESTINE told her something was wrong. The dopey goat was always first to butt her nose in where she wasn't wanted, and now she stopped trying to steal Maggie's seaweed and raised her nose to stare.

The aeroplane was stalling, dropping towards the sea, fighting its way up again, but then dropping closer. It was being forced to land, Maggie thought incredulously, but there was no safe landing strip here. Listall Island was two miles long and a mile wide, it had some of the most spectacular scenery in Australia, but there was no flat land for its entire length.

'They'll be killed,' Maggie gasped. Her voice trailed off as the plane banked sharply against the wind, lurched in an over-correction to its other side—and headed downward out of sight.

She heard no crash, but maybe she was too far away. She might not have seen the plane at all if Ernestine hadn't stared.

Now the faint sound of sick engine died to an echo and the island wind once again filled her ears. Ernestine stared upward for half a second longer, then turned back to Maggie's kelp as if the drama was played out.

Maggie left her to it. With her dog at her side, but feeling more isolated than she'd felt in her life before, she started to run.

The plane trouble was the last of a series of disasters, and Dev Macafferty couldn't believe it was happening.

First there had been trouble with the aunts. Between them, his two aunts had the force of a major tornado, and their retirement to 'look after dear Devlin' had been a disaster from the start.

Dev had been trying to sort that when the call had come from his ex-wife. 'I'm leaving for the States tomorrow, Devlin, and Dominic has been expelled from school. There's no way he's coming with us, so you'll get what you've always wanted. The brat's yours.'

The brat. Dominic. His son, whom he'd hardly seen since birth. His son, whom he'd ached for...

Aside from his hassles with the aunts, Dev also had a problem with his company. The value of the Australian dollar was falling, finance had to be restructured and the company accountants were pulling their hair. It couldn't matter. Dominic needed him...

So he'd made soothing noises to the aunts—gee, that had helped!—then caught the first flight to Sydney, to find Dominic hadn't been expelled at all. The headmaster was simply asking that he leave.

'We don't feel boarding school is suitable for your son,' Dev had been told. 'We agree to take young children if they're well adjusted, with sensible reasons for boarding, but Dominic's not a well-adjusted eight-year-old. His only friend seems to be his computer. It's our opinion that he's been seriously neglected, and it's your job to fix that. Not ours.'

Dev had winced, but he hadn't been able to defend himself. Somehow he'd managed to stay calm, collect the one meagre suitcase of Dom's belongings and take the little boy back to the airport.

Where on earth to start? He didn't know, but his first priority must be to get Dom back to Tasmania. Maybe the aunts could funnel their tornado energy into helping. Or maybe...maybe he didn't have a clue!

Then had come the next problem. He'd walked into the airport to find all commercial flights grounded, due to a pilots' strike.

Things had gotten way out of hand. His mobile phone had kept ringing. Where the hell was he? his people had demanded. His accountants' hair must be almost non-existent by now.

There had been one silver lining to this mess. Dev had his pilot's licence, but it had taken hours of negotiating and influence to find a plane for hire. Everyone had wanted a plane.

'It won't be much longer,' he'd promised Dominic between phone calls, but his small son had been indifferent.

'Why are we going to Tasmania anyway?' Dominic had demanded fretfully, clutching his school bag as if it was his lifeline. 'I bet you can't even get an internet connection in Tasmania.'

Dev had looked down at this dark little replica of himself and felt dazed. How on earth could he answer that? This was his son and he didn't know the first thing about him. What had the headmaster said? *Neglected!* In what way? His gut had churned at the thought.

Finally he'd found a plane for hire and they'd taken off. In the air, Dominic had been silent, staring straight ahead in stoic indifference. Dev had tried to talk, but it had been like talking to wood. This wasn't going to be easy!

And now...

Getting to know Dominic, the problems of his company and the hassles with the aunts all faded into insignificance. They were a hundred miles from land, his first engine had failed and the second engine was stalling.

'What's happening?' Dominic asked, in the tone of a

child who knew he didn't have to worry—the adults of his world would take care of things. Dev glanced down at his small son, and there was ice in his heart.

He couldn't crash. Not now, not when he'd been given this amazing chance at fatherhood... He couldn't!

The island loomed out of nowhere and Dev let his breath out with a whistle of relief. He'd forgotten about Listall. He turned urgently to the radio, but his relief was short-lived.

'There's no landing strip on Listall,' the controller told him, his voice calm against Dev's urgency. 'There's not even a road. King Island's your closest...'

The engine coughed again and the plane sank. Dev fought it back to life and nosed the plane upward, but it coughed and sank again.

'It's no good,' he said grimly into the microphone. 'I'm going down.'

'You can't.' The controller dropped his calm and his panic matched Dev's. 'Permission denied. There's nothing...'

'Dominic, put your head between your knees and cover your head with your arms,' Dev said fiercely. 'There's no choice. I'm landing!'

Maggie tore around the last rocky outcrop and stopped dead. The plane had landed at the far end of the beach. Deeply gouged wheel marks showed it had skidded and skewed wildly on the loose sand, and it had almost made it. If the beach had been ten yards longer, then maybe it would have, but the jutting granite outcrop had spelled defeat. The nose cone had smashed deep into rock.

But the cockpit was still almost intact. As Maggie stared in horror, a small boy stumbled down from the passenger's side. He was about eight years old and dressed in school uniform; he had black, curly hair and his face was white with fear. Maggie took a deep breath and stepped forward to reach him. There was smoke billowing from the crumpled metal and the child looked stunned, but otherwise he seemed unhurt.

She had no time to comfort him. The smoke was growing denser by the minute. 'Let's get you clear,' Maggie said fiercely, hauling the child into her arms and pulling him away. If the plane exploded now... 'Who else is in there?' she demanded. There was no time even to be kind. She had to know!

'Only...my computer, and...'

'And?'

'My...my dad's in there,' the little boy said, and his voice was surprisingly strong as he held himself rigid in her arms. 'My father's the same as me. His name's Devlin Macafferty.' Amazingly there was even a trace of pride in the child's voice as she pulled him away. 'I'm Dominic. D. Macafferty. My father's Devlin Macafferty, so he's D. Macafferty, too. We're the same.'

Maggie blinked, and had to force herself back to the important issue as she ran. 'Your father's the pilot?'

'Yes.'

'Dominic, are there any other passengers in the plane?' She was running with him as she spoke, breathing hard and hauling him away to the other side of the granite outcrop with a speed she hadn't known she was capable of.

'N...no.'

'You're sure? Just you and your dad?'

'Yes.'

'Good boy.' She planted him unceremoniously on the sand, out of sight of the plane. Please Lord, let it not explode... 'Don't move,' she ordered. 'Not one inch.' He desperately needed comfort, but there was no time! 'Lucy, stay,' she ordered her shaggy black and white collie. 'Dominic, stay with Lucy!'—and she left him at a run.

Back at the plane, the smoke was increasing so much she could hardly see. Don't let it go up, she prayed. Please... Give me time...

The pilot's door was smashed into rock. Hopeless! One look had her running back to the door Dominic had climbed from. She took one more fearful look at the billowing black smoke, sucked in a lungful of smoke-filled air—and clambered up into the cockpit.

The pilot was still at the controls. The crash must have knocked him unconscious, but he was starting to come round. As Maggie reached him, he opened dazed eyes and stared upward.

There was no mistaking this man as the child's father. The resemblance was almost uncanny, though the man was far more battered than the child. There was blood oozing from a jagged cut on his strongly boned face, and there was pain in his eyes. As Maggie searched his face he put his fingers up, as if to find the source of the hurt. 'What the...?'

Once again, there was no time for comfort. 'You need to get out,' Maggie said urgently, choking on smoke. Her fingers fought the seat-belt clip at his waist and, blessedly, it unclicked in her fingers. 'Now.'

'But I don't... I don't....'

The cut on his forehead was deep. He'd obviously had a major thump but there was no time to worry. Maggie's eyes were searching the smoke-filled cabin to check his legs weren't trapped. No... They seemed clear.

'Who are you?' he managed.

This was hardly the time for introductions. 'You have to get out!' she snapped, and then, as he closed his eyes again, she raised her voice. 'No. Don't close your eyes. You get out *now*!' Her hands seized his arm and hauled him sideways, but he was too big for her to drag across the cockpit—not when his feet were still under the control panel. He had to help. Please let him not lose consciousness again...

She pulled, but he didn't shift. His eyes flickered and closed again...

'The plane's about to burn,' she screamed. 'Move!' She gasped in a lungful of smoke-filled air, but there was no time to cough. 'Move!'

'My...' His eyes flickered open.

'Move!' The man was only half conscious. Maggie put her arms around his chest—he felt like a steel-strutted barrel—and hauled for all she was worth. *'Pull your legs up!'* she yelled. The way she was yelling she'd almost deafen him, but the alternative was worse. *'Help me!'*

And finally she got through. He blinked once, stared outward at the shattered cockpit and then seemed to collect himself, hauling his legs upward.

He didn't have to pull far. With his legs free, she could move him. Before he knew it, he was being dragged sideways, and Maggie didn't stop. She hauled herself out of the plane, falling downwards and dragging him headfirst after her, until they landed in a heap of tangled limbs on the sand.

Even then she didn't falter. She was up almost as they hit the sand, hauling him backward. 'You're not safe yet,' she yelled. 'Move. Come on, move...'

'My son!' The fog was clearing, and the horror was flooding back. There was blood oozing from the cut on his face and Dev put a hand up as if to clear his eyes. His body was limp on the sand. He coughed and struggled to push her back from him. 'Dominic... He's in...'

'Your son's safe. But you'll kill us both if you stay here.'

In desperation, Maggie seized and yanked on a thick thatch of black curls, hauling him upward. 'Move!'

'*Ow…*'

'I'll hurt you more than that if you don't shift.' She shoved a hand under his arm and yanked. 'Run! Your son's safe, but you have to run!' Maybe he'd broken both legs, she thought desperately, but even then she didn't care. She couldn't shift him without help. Broken legs or not, he had to move!

Somehow he did. As Dev lurched to his feet, Maggie's slim frame dived under his shoulder in support, and they half stumbled, half ran the few steps around the outcrop.

Five seconds later, the plane exploded into a roaring ball of flame.

It was minutes before anyone spoke. Dev collapsed on the sand and so did Maggie, her breath coming in painful, ragged gasps as her smoke-filled lungs struggled to recover. They'd come so close… The sound of the fire was all around them, and the stink of burning fuel filled the air. One minute more…

Don't think about it.

Finally Maggie recovered enough to make her shocked brain work. They were safe enough now, and the fire couldn't last. It had exploded with such force and was now burning so fiercely that it must soon be over. Maggie hauled herself up to join Dominic. The little boy was staring, mesmerised, at the burning plane. She placed her arm around his trembling shoulders, and her arm was none too steady either.

'It's okay, Dominic,' she managed across the roar of the flame. She pulled him in close to her, shielding him from the heat, but his thin little body was stiff and unyielding, and his face was still deathly white. 'You're okay and so is your dad.' She cast a look back to where the man was lying on the sand behind them. His eyes were closed again, but he'd run. He had to be okay. She'd check, but first...

'Dominic, are you sure there was no one else aboard?' she asked gently, and held her breath. It was too late now—but if he'd been wrong...

'No.' The boy gulped and blinked back tears. 'But my laptop computer was in my schoolbag.'

'Oh... Oh, dear.' Somehow that was too much. It was almost impossible to choke back laughter that was almost hysterical, but somehow she managed it. The loss of his laptop, by the sound of it, was a major source of grief, but if all they'd lost was a computer...

'You know, I wouldn't be surprised if the plane's insured,' she said unsteadily. 'You'll be able to buy a new laptop.'

'But I just got *Flight Warrior*. Sam Craigiburn put this version on my hard disk and I can't get it again.'

Oh, heck...

'I...I'll just go check that your dad's okay,' Maggie said weakly, and left him to his grief. There were some sorrows she couldn't share, and just now she didn't have the strength to try. Concentrate on priorities, she told herself helplessly—not computer games. See to the boy's father!

Devlin Macafferty was lying flat on the sand, and for the first time now Maggie really looked at him. He seemed in his mid-thirties, and, by the look of him, not a man to mess with. The man was large, lean, like his son, but superbly muscled, with dark, aquiline features and thick black hair in unruly curls.

While she'd hauled him out, shouted at him and ordered him around, Maggie had caught a flash of gorgeous deep brown eyes which linked man and boy together even more firmly. Dominic's eyes were just that shade of brown.

But then Maggie glanced uneasily back at Dominic.

While the man was lying seemingly unconscious on the sand, the child was mourning his computer. He'd spoken of his father with pride, but now he hardly seemed concerned about him. Something didn't make sense.

Devlin's eyes flickered open again. He was conscious, Maggie knew, but the effort of opening his eyes to sunlight must be almost too great an effort to bear. This was *some* thump on the head. The bruise around the cut was swelling while she watched.

Maybe there was internal bleeding, she thought fearfully, a new horror looming. If there was an intracranial bleed…

Don't think about that now! If anything was in the too hard basket, that was. She put her fingers on Dev's forehead, pushed a stray curl back from his cut and tried a reassuring smile down into those gorgeous eyes. It wouldn't help to let him see panic.

'It's okay,' she told him softly, seeing him wince. 'There's no rush now. Close your eyes again if you like. Dominic's safe.'

'The plane…' His eyes widened rather than closed.

'The plane's fast turning to a pile of ash. There's nothing you can do to stop it.'

'But if you hadn't come…'

'Hey, isn't it lucky I did?' She smiled down at his worried face and managed a twinkle. 'Ernestine told me there was trouble, so here I am. Thank Ernestine, not me.'

'Who's Ernestine?'

'A goat. Speaking of which…' A clatter of stones from above made her look up, and she grinned. 'Here comes the cavalry.' Eight feet above them, lined up on the bluff, was the milking herd, staring down at the scene before them with astonishment. Ernestine Goat with thirty of her cronies. Dev's eyes widened.

'*This* is the cavalry?' he asked weakly.

'Yep. Commander Ernestine and her troops, checking to see if there's anything edible. Hey, you don't have to get up. My goats won't annoy the casualties.'

But Dev was pushing himself to his feet, and by the look on his face he was pushing back pain. It wasn't just his head, Maggie thought as she watched him rise. His leg?

If it was, he wasn't admitting it. 'If I'm the worst there is, there are no casualties,' he said firmly, with a swift, sideways glance to where Dominic was watching his computer's funeral pyre. 'If the goats are after roast dinner, then they'll be disappointed—thanks to you.'

He put out his hand and took hers. 'I'm Devlin Macafferty, and I can't tell you how pleased I am to meet you.' He hesitated, and then shook his head, as though shaking off a nightmare. 'Fifteen minutes ago I didn't think I'd be meeting anyone ever again.'

'It was a pretty stupid place to land,' Maggie agreed, smiling to take away implied criticism. The man's grip was warm, strong and sure, and Maggie looked up into his eyes and felt her insides give a strange little jump—as if something had just shifted… She blinked, and then caught herself. 'I…we're a bit short in the tarmac department on this island.'

'I noticed that.' He wasn't as tough as he was making out, Maggie thought. Even though he was trying to smile, there was a tremor underneath his deep voice. 'I hardly had a choice where I put down.'

'I guessed that.' She was watching the pain in his eyes with concern. Still her hand lay in his, as if he was unconscious of it—or as if he needed the human contact. 'You've hurt your head, but is there anything else wrong? You look like you're hurting.'

'I'll live.' He managed a lop-sided smile and his grip on

her hand tightened. 'Thanks to you. Can I ask who you are?'

'I'm Maggie Cray,' she told him, hauling her hand back and shoving it into her jeans pocket—a defensive and stupid gesture she didn't understand herself 'My dog's name is Lucy, and the goats are led by Ernestine. Individual introductions to the girls can wait—but we're all very pleased to see you intact, even though you've made an awful mess of our beach.'

She was talking too fast, she thought strangely, and why on earth did she still feel so weird? Maggie moved away, so she could stare back along the sand—and so she could stop looking at him and fight off the weird sensations his smile was causing. 'You've wasted an awful lot of our bull kelp,' she added, inconsequentially.

'I beg your pardon?'

'We collect bull kelp,' she told him. Reaction was setting in with her, too. She should be warm enough in her windcheater and jeans, but suddenly she found herself shivering, and she couldn't make herself look back at him. A sudden vision engulfed her of what might have been—if she hadn't looked up to see what Ernestine was staring at or if she hadn't run so fast—and she felt sick to the core. If she hadn't come...

She had. That was all that mattered—so talk about something else. The bull kelp... Talk about bull kelp.

'Now my kelp has petrol fumes and ash all through it and it'll be useless,' she managed.

'What do you use bull kelp for?' Dev said faintly, and Maggie managed to smile at his tone. He sounded as if he thought she ate it.

'Ancient witchcraft rituals,' she couldn't resist saying. 'Dead of night stuff, with dead cats, incense, full moons and the odd skull or two.' Then, at his look of absolute confusion, she relented. She might be feeling strange, but he must be feeling crazy. To have been so close to death...

'Actually, we dry it and export it to Scotland, where one of the big pharmaceutical companies turns it into medicines. I only keep a little for ritualistic purposes—like disposal of nose warts and turning people into frogs.'

Then she turned to look at Dominic, who was still staring at the fire, his small frame rigid. 'I think...if you're fit to walk...then it's time to get you to the house,' she told his father. 'Could you...?' She motioned to Dominic, and the implication was obvious. The little boy needed contact.

Dev nodded. He took the few steps to where his son was standing and Maggie's eyes creased as she saw him walk. He *had* hurt his leg.

'Dom?' he said.

There was no answer.

'Dominic, we'll take you to the house now,' Dev said softly. 'This is Maggie and she'll help us.'

'My computer's burned.'

'I'll buy you another.'

'It was *my* computer,' Dominic said savagely, turning on him in fury. '*Mine!* I won it in a competition and it's mine!'

'I understand that.' Dev put his hand around the little boy's shoulders but he was shoved away.

'Leave me alone. You've burned my computer.'

'Dominic, let's go to the house.'

'No. Leave me alone.'

'We have to go, Dom...'

Maggie caught her breath. She looked from father and son, and both their faces were rigid.

For Dev, the pain and shock were setting in hard, Maggie thought. He was at the end of his rope, and he didn't seem to have a clue how to treat his son.

Well, maybe she could help. She did know about treating

shocked kids, and she had a great tool right at hand. She clicked her fingers to call Lucy, and led the collie to where Dominic was standing.

'Dominic, I'm Maggie,' she said gently. 'And this is my very best friend, Lucy. Lucy, shake hands.'

In answer, Lucy looked up at Dominic, her intelligent eyes a question.

'Lucy, shake,' Maggie said again.

The collie placed her head on one side, checked Dominic out from the toes up, then obediently sank her rear haunches on the ground and raised a paw.

Most kids couldn't resist. Maggie herself had never been able to, though Lucy shook hands with her on average fifty times a day, but Dominic tried. For a whole minute he stood rigid, unmoving, with his father standing helplessly at his side.

The child looked down at the dog, and then tried looking away, but Lucy wasn't having a bar of it. She stayed exactly where she was, right in front of him, her eyes resting firmly on his, her shaggy tail moving seductively back and forth and her paw outstretched.

The moment stretched on, and there was absolute silence. Dev glanced at Maggie, but Maggie shook her head. Don't interfere, her eyes told him, and the man was smart enough to realise he shouldn't. So he held his breath. Dominic looked down at Lucy, and then away again—and then back…

Lucy's tail kept right on wagging.

And finally it was too much to resist. Dominic held out his hand and, very solemnly, took Lucy's pad in his fingers. Lucy's bushy tail wagged even more as Dominic gravely shook hands—and then Lucy did what Maggie had known she would do, what she'd tried hard to train her not to, but to no avail. She jumped up on her hind legs, put two paws firmly on Dominic's shoulders, and licked from jaw to fore-head.

Dominic gave one long, convulsive shudder—put his arms around the dog and burst into tears.

Somehow they made it back to the house, though it was a strange procession, with Maggie's shoulder supporting Dev as he limped, her hand firmly holding Dominic's, and with Lucy wedged tight on the child's other side—plus thirty goats bringing up the rear.

By the time they reached the house, Dev was grey-faced with pain. He was barely taking in his surroundings, and he sank down in the back bedroom as if he'd never rise again.

Maggie was incredibly glad to see him there. She was starting to worry a lot about his head injury.

'I'll radio Melbourne and tell them you're here,' she told him. 'Air traffic must know you've gone down.'

'Yeah,' he agreed weakly. His head was bleeding slug-gishly but he didn't appear to notice any more—and Mag-gie thought a stained pillow was the least of her worries. 'Thank you. I radioed I was in trouble. They'll be wor-ried…'

'I'll let them know we need medical help and they'll send a helicopter to evacuate you. You need X-rays to make sure there's no intracranial bleed…'

'Hey, I've bled enough on the surface,' Dev said faintly. 'I'm not bleeding inside.'

'We don't know that until you're checked.'

'There's a cheery note.' Dev managed a smile across at his son, who was standing, white-faced, at the door, with Lucy still by his side. 'Don't listen to her, Dominic. If I'd managed to do any real damage, my headache would be getting worse—not better. I might look bloodstained and battle-scarred, but your father will live.'

Dominic simply stared blankly at him, as if it didn't matter either way. Which, come to think of it, from the way he was acting…

'I'll go and call,' Maggie interrupted. 'I'll come back and help you into bed in a minute, and I'll do something about that cut then. But if I don't call now we'll have Air Sea Rescue planes coming from the mainland, when what I want is a helicopter.''

'I don't need to get into bed—and I don't need a helicopter,' Dev said bluntly. 'Tell them the plane's crashed but we're fine.'

'But I want your head X-rayed,' Maggie told him.

'I don't,' Dev said firmly, and met her look. 'And it's my head.'

'I saved it for you,' Maggie said belligerently. 'If it wasn't for me it'd be roast head.'

'So that gives you photograph rights?'

'Yes.' She tilted her chin, and, despite the pain in his head, he managed a smile.

'Then you should have made me sign a contract before you saved me.' Enough of humour. It was too much effort. He gave a faint groan and closed his eyes. 'Honestly, Miss Cray, there's no need to fuss. I know I look dreadful, but it's only blood. I intend to live, and I want no Air Sea Rescue efforts on my behalf. So…if you have such a thing as an ice pack, an aspirin and a piece of sticking plaster, I would be eternally grateful—and if you could take care of Dominic while I pull myself together I would also appreciate it. But otherwise…please…just let me be.'

His eyes met hers, steel meeting steel. Maggie blinked. She was a strong enough personality, but this man was stronger. He was accustomed to command, she thought—accustomed to getting his own way.

Well, it was *his* head, she told herself helplessly. If he wanted to die...

'If I die in the next twenty-four hours I've left enough insurance for Dominic to buy another computer,' Devlin said grimly, as if reading her thoughts. 'That's all that matters, and otherwise I won't be missed. But honestly, Miss Cray, I have no intention of dying. Just give me the ice pack and let me be.'

Maggie stared down, her eyes still troubled.

'Come on, Maggie,' he said softly, seeing her indecision. 'I'm a grown man. Give me my aspirin and let me sleep. Concentrate on Dominic. He needs you. I don't.'

CHAPTER TWO

WHEN Dev woke it was dark. For a moment he didn't have a clue where he was. He lay with his eyes closed while the day's events came flooding back. Then he ventured to open his eyes a fraction and check.

The dark was lessened by one candle, sitting in the window embrasure. In its light sat a girl.

Maggie…

The name whispered into his mind with pleasure, and somehow calmed the jagged ache in his head and leg. This was Maggie—the girl who'd saved his life.

She was like no woman he'd ever met before, he thought dazedly. This afternoon she'd been in torn jeans, a windcheater way too big for her and her brown curls caught up in some sort of twist at the top. She'd looked like a kid, he remembered, with too many freckles, a nose that was definitely snub, and clear green eyes that twinkled. She'd looked about fifteen.

But tonight… Tonight she didn't look fifteen. She looked mature and serene and very, very lovely.

Lovely? Yes, he was right to call her that, he thought, but she was lovely in a way Dev wasn't accustomed to. The women he spent time with were usually gorgeous, sophisticated, and clothed with no expense spared. Tonight, Maggie was dressed in homespun. She was wearing a loose flowing crimson skirt that reached her ankles, a soft cream blouse and a hand-knit shawl, and her curls floated down around her shoulders in a soft cloud. She looked like something out of an old fashion cameo…

'Staring is rude,' she said softly, and the spell was broken.

'I thought I might have died and been transported back a century or two,' he told her, managing a smile as she rose and crossed to the bed. 'You look like you've stepped straight out of *Jane Eyre*.'

Amazingly, she didn't blush or appear the least self-conscious. 'You like my skirt?' Maggie paused on her way to the bed and whirled in a full circle, causing her skirt to flare out around her. 'I spun it and wove it myself, and I'm *so* proud of it. It took ages.'

'It's great,' Dev said blankly, and Maggie grinned.

'Yeah, well, maybe it isn't. It's great by candlelight, but in fact it's full of pulls and flaws and the dye is patchy—but for a first attempt it's not bad, and I only wear it at night. The company here's limited, so I don't get much criticism. How are you feeling?'

Dev thought about that for a bit, and there was only one way to describe it. 'Lousy,' he admitted.

'Your head's really bad?' It was impossible to disguise the anxiety in her tone and Dev winced. He had her really worried, then. Maybe it would have been better to get the helicopter out to evacuate them. He'd caused enough trouble...

'My head's fine. I told you, I'm not going to die on you.' Then, at the look on her face, he relented. 'Well, maybe it's not fine, but it's definitely better.'

'I'm very pleased to hear it.' Maggie's anxiety took a step back and she smiled serenely at him. 'I might be a qualified nurse but I make a lousy gravedigger. This ground's rock hard. I have a lot of trouble when one of my goats dies, and you're twice as big!'

'Yeah?' The thought of this girl digging graves on her rocky island was almost too much. Dev blinked, and it took a huge effort to haul himself back to reality. But there was a worry…

'Dominic?' There was no mistaking the anxiety in *his* voice this time. 'How is he? He didn't seem hurt.'

'He's not,' Maggie told him. 'He's only shocked. He ate some dinner and he's asleep now, with Lucy beside him. He's had a sob about his computer, but Lucy's sticking close. For tonight I'm putting aside nursing principles that says pillows shouldn't be shared with dogs.'

'You're a…are you really a nurse?' He stared and Maggie grinned.

'Why shouldn't I be a nurse?'

'Well, for a start,' Dev said cautiously, 'I don't see any hospital.'

'I trained in Melbourne. Basic training, followed by obstetrics, paediatrics, emergency medicine and psychology. Anything you care to throw at me…'

'So why are you here?'

'This is my home,' she said simply. 'But nursing is what I'm trained to do, and I'm about to do some now. Mr Macafferty, I need to put a few stitches in that cut on your head.'

'It's Dev…and you're kidding.' Instinctively Dev put his hand to the dressing on his head and winced. The thought of someone touching it…

'I won't hurt.'

'They always say that.'

'"They", as in doctors?'

'No, "they" as in my old school nurse when she gave us injections. You use just the same tone.'

'They teach us the tone in nursing school,' Maggie said smugly. She lifted a box of matches from the bedside table and then applied herself to lighting a kerosene lamp. The wick flickered and caught, and the room filled with a soft glow. In its light Maggie looked more beautiful than ever. 'Come on, let me sew you up or I'll call in the cavalry,' she said.

'You mean the goats?'

'Actually, I meant the ambulance helicopter from the mainland, but come to think of it the goats might be just as good a threat. How do you feel about thirty goats in your bedroom?' She bent down and flicked open a case beside his bed. 'Come on, Mr Macafferty, twenty stitches or thirty goats. Which will it be?'

'I don't need twenty stitches.'

'I'll do it in eighteen, then,' she said kindly, meeting his eyes with good-humoured determination. Nurse humouring recalcitrant patient... 'Honest, it does need to be done, and I'm more than capable of doing it. If I leave it like it is, you'll end up with a scar an inch wide. I should have stitched it before, but the bleeding had slowed to almost nothing. I was worried about Dominic, and I didn't want to do anything until I'd convinced myself you weren't dying of internal haemorrhage.'

'And I'm not?'

'What do you reckon?' She grinned. 'I'd still like an X-ray, but your vital signs are fine. I've been checking you every fifteen minutes.'

'Yeah?' Dev lay back on his pillows and let that sink in. The thought of this woman checking on him every fifteen minutes—while he'd been out like a light—was strangely unnerving. Weird. 'You've been checking my vital signs. Like...what?'

'Well, whether you were breathing or not,' Maggie said cheerfully. 'That always seems a good start. But your blood pressure's been okay, too...'

'You've checked my blood pressure?'

'Mmm,' Maggie agreed. 'You'll be pleased to know you

seem strong as a horse—so I did what you wanted and told the ambulance boys not to bother coming. Which they're really relieved about because there's been a major road trauma up in the high country on the mainland. It seems, with the plane strike, every fool in the country is trying to kill themselves with alternative ways of getting home.'

'Is that what you think I am? A fool?'

'I have absolutely no idea what you are, Mr Macafferty,' she said primly, lifting a syringe from her medical case and snapping off a vial of anaesthetic.

'Devlin.'

'Mr Macafferty until I've stitched you.'

Dev gave up. 'You really are qualified to handle that thing?' Dev said nervously, eyeing the needle.

'I'm a fine needlewoman. You were the one who admired my skirt.'

'I'm not looking at frills and neat hemlines, here.'

'Nope. You're looking at a clean wound and a hairline scar. Trust me, Mr Macafferty.'

'Dev, or I won't.'

'Dev, then.' She smiled down at him in the soft light. 'Okay, Dev, I have no idea what you are, and you don't know the first thing about me, but maybe we have to take each other on trust. So…just lie back and think of England and let me do my worst.'

He stared up into her clear green eyes and there was a moment of absolute silence. Take her on trust, she'd said, and he had no choice. Trust her?

'Okay, Miss Cray,' he said softly.

'Maggie.'

'Maggie, then.' He smiled up into those intense, clear eyes and he knew that he did. Her eyes were direct and warm and honest, and absolutely without deceit.

It was like a wash of sea foam, he thought blankly, crystal-clear, and cool and absolutely pure. A woman like no other…

'Can I start?' she asked softly, and he caught himself with an effort.

'Yes.'

'You trust me?'

'I have no choice.'

'Nope,' she agreed blithely. 'I have a medical monopoly on the island. I can charge what I like. How very nice.' And she loaded her vial and carefully inserted her needle.

Maggie firstly anaesthetised the area, then carefully cleaned and finally sutured the jagged tear. It took her about half an hour, her eyes a mirror of intense concentration and her face only inches from his.

She didn't speak, and when Dev tried to break the silence she shook her head. No way. She couldn't talk to him and concentrate at the same time.

She might talk confidently, but in truth Maggie was anything but. It was usually doctors who sewed wounds. Maggie had seen it done hundreds of times, but she'd only ever assisted. When she'd come to the island she'd brought a full complement of medical supplies, but she'd hoped with all her heart that she wouldn't need to use them…

Now, however, there seemed little choice.

Finally it was over. Maggie drew a deep breath, rose and stepped back, then closed her eyes and ran a weary hand across her face, letting Dev see for the first time that she'd been under even more strain than him. She bit her lip and bent to find a dressing, and when she rose she had her face under control again, but he'd seen…

'Thank you, Maggie,' he said softly, and her pale face flushed.

'It was nothing.'

'I appreciate it.'

'Wait until you see your scar. I might have done it in herringbone stitch.'

'Then I'll look in the mirror and remember you always,' he quipped lightly, but Maggie's flush deepened.

'Don't. You needed a surgeon.'

Dev put tentative fingers up and ran them across the still anaesthetised wound. Even he could tell that the scar was finely drawn together—no mean feat, considering she hadn't even a decent light.

'It's fine. I doubt if a surgeon with anaesthetist and nurses and theatre lights could have done better. You don't have electricity here?'

'It's a bit far to run a cable from the mainland.' The strain over, Maggie almost had herself under control again, and her flush was fading. She came back to the bed and gently applied a dressing. Her fingers were light and tender and warm on his forehead, and once again Dev had to pinch himself to keep his grip on reality. In these clothes…in these surroundings…she was…surreal?

'We have a generator, but with no lights attached,' she told him, placing her last piece of sticking plaster in place. 'Fuel's too precious for luxuries like lighting. Our power's for the refrigerators only.'

Refrigerators. He hadn't thought a woman like this would need anything so mundane. 'So we can get cold beer?' he asked.

'Cold milk only.' She grinned. 'Sorry, beer's off the list of what you can get on this island. I can supply whisky, but even that's not available until tomorrow. You're not touching alcohol tonight.'

'No, ma'am.'

'I could give you a cup of tea,' she said, relenting.

Dev shook his head. Weariness was washing over him

in waves and his head was still dully aching. Half the reason he was reacting to Maggie the way he was must be because of the bang on his head, he thought dazedly. It must be. He motioned to the glass of water by his bedside. 'This is fine,' he told her. 'It's all I need. If you don't mind…'

'You'd just like to sleep.' Maggie nodded. She flipped a couple of tablets from a bottle and handed them over. 'Take these. They're painkillers, and they'll help your leg as well as your head.'

'My leg?' He'd almost forgotten his leg was hurting. Almost, but not quite.

'You have a massive bruise on your upper thigh,' she told him. 'Don't you remember? I hauled your pants off when I put you to bed and had a look.'

'You didn't!'

'Okay, I didn't.' She grinned. 'I know, you told me to go away and leave you to die, but I couldn't actually do that unless I'd convinced myself there was every chance you'd live. So I radioed Melbourne that you were safe and then I came back to check. You were almost asleep, but you didn't make any protest when I undressed you.'

Dev's jaw dropped. He hadn't noticed until now, but he put his hand down under the covers and there were bare legs… Bare chest…

His jocks were still present, he thought incredulously. Thank heaven for small mercies….

'I am a nurse,' Maggie said softly, smiling at his shocked expression. 'Undressing semi-conscious patients is one of my skills—and if you're worried about a chaperon, Dominic and Lucy were present all the time. Dominic was very impressed with your bruise.'

'I'll bet he was.' Good grief, by the sound of it he'd be the last person to see his own injury. He felt an almost instinctive urge to pick up the covers and peer down at the source of his leg pain, but somehow he controlled it. He looked up to find Maggie's smile had grown even wider. She'd guessed what he was thinking.

'Go on—have a look.'

'No way.' He was shy, for heaven's sake. He was absurdly self-conscious about pushing back the covers and exposing himself almost naked in front of this woman…and she was the one who'd undressed him!

Maggie chuckled at the look on his face, and his discomfort intensified. 'I'll leave the lamp burning when I go,' she told him, finally taking pity on his confoundment. 'Look all you like. I wouldn't worry, though. The way you were walking, I was concerned you might have dislocated or broken something, so I had to check, but, even though it looks awful, a haematoma will go away all by itself. Given time.'

'I…' Damn, he was totally disconcerted.

'Don't worry. Just sleep,' she said softly, bending over and pulling the bedclothes up to his chin—just like a mother tucking in a child. It was a weird, maternal gesture that had Dev's insides doing handstands. He felt totally, crazily at sea in the presence of this woman.

He couldn't think—but it seemed he didn't have to. 'You just sleep, Dev Macafferty,' she told him. 'For now, your world is safe. Worry about tomorrow tomorrow. For now, just sleep.'

And she smiled warmly down at him—then lifted the candle from the window embrasure and floated out in her crazy homespun skirt, with her mass of wonderful curls floating after her.

Dev woke to the sound of the sea, and a pain-free world.

Nothing. Nothing, nothing and nothing.

For a while he lay absolutely still, glorying in the fact that his head had stopped its grinding ache of the night before. He opened his eyes wider, waiting for the pain to start again, but there was nothing.

Glory be.

He tested his leg. That was a bit of a mistake. The pain hadn't completely gone, then. It was hanging around, ready to strike, but if he lay still…

Maggie had been back some time during the night—probably doing her vital-sign testing again. Well, he was still breathing, he thought grimly. What else did the woman want? There were two more pills and a fresh tumbler of water on his bedside table. Dev took them with gratitude, then lay back and soaked in his surroundings while he waited for the pills to take effect.

This was an amazing house, but he'd hardly noticed the night before. It seemed ancient, with sagging window sashes, no curtains, and cracks in the whitewashed walls. It was sparsely furnished, but the sun was glistening in through a clean window, the white coverlet on the cast-iron bed was spotless and the ancient wooden floorboards were polished rich with age.

It was so Spartan he might well be in a monastery.

There was a walking stick resting by the bedhead. Courtesy of Maggie, he supposed, and wondered what else the woman was capable of producing? Medical kit? Walking sticks? Shovels for gravedigging?

Dev grinned—and then eyed the stick with caution. In a few minutes when the tablets had worked then maybe he'd give it a try. There were clothes on the bed-end: loose fisherman's pants and a jersey ready to go. Good grief! Her organisation was amazing—but he wasn't sure he wanted to go anywhere.

There was no sound apart from the sea, and after a while

Dev found it unnerving. There had to be some sound from somewhere.

He needed to go the bathroom…

She hadn't thought of that, he thought, and grimaced— and then grinned again. If she had, then he wouldn't have put it past the redoubtable Maggie to set up a catheter…

Thank heaven for small mercies. That indignity at least had been spared him.

The minutes rolled on, and finally the jarring pain in his leg settled. He moved it experimentally in the bed, winced and moved it again, but this time it was better. Okay, by the look of the pile of clothes and the walking stick, Maggie obviously thought he could get up. He wouldn't let the lady down.

Maggie…

The name stayed with him, drifting in and out of his thoughts, and he felt himself stir at the thought of her. The reaction made him frown. It was a long time since a woman had affected him like this.

A long time? This reaction wasn't just physical, he thought, remembering the look of her in the candlelight the night before. Her touch… The smell of her…

In truth, he couldn't remember feeling this way about someone ever. It wasn't that she was extraordinarily lovely or witty or…or anything. In his normal business settings she'd look like a fish out of water, and maybe…if he saw her coming across a hotel lobby towards him he'd probably grimace. He liked his women well groomed, and homespun was all very well for an island…

Homespun was all very well for a sick man's fancy, he told himself harshly, but as for real life…

In real life, Maggie was clearly expecting him to get out of bed, and a man had some pride. He winced and got on with it, but it took ten minutes to get himself decent. Thankfully there wasn't a mirror in the room, so he just had to guess what his face looked like—in fact, if he'd seen how sick he looked he might have climbed right back under the covers and stayed. But somewhere outside there was Dominic, and a whole new chance...

Once he'd limped out his bedroom door, Maggie's organisation hit home again. A note on the opposite wall told him where to go. Kitchen to the right, down a stone-floored passage that looked more like a tunnel. Bathroom to the left...

He spent a bad few minutes in the bathroom, staring at the mirror and trying to decide just what he might look like when the swelling went down—and whether he wanted to wash in the ice cold water from the single tap—and, no, there was no way he was going to shave—and then, finally, leaning heavily on his walking stick, Dev limped to the kitchen.

He'd expected to find Maggie or Dominic, or at least Lucy. What he found was someone who looked more like a weathered gnome.

The old man was hunched in a vast armchair beside the wood stove, his frame curved with age. He looked about a hundred, Dev thought blankly, but the old eyes that turned to his were alive and young, and twinkling with the same green light he'd seen in Maggie's.

'Well, well...' The gnome didn't rise, but his alert old eyes checked Dev from the toes up. 'If it isn't Maggie's driftwood. I'm Joseph Cray, Maggie's grandfather. You must be Devlin Macafferty, father to young Dominic. That's my sweater you're wearing, and my pants. Lucky I wear them long. They don't look too bad on you at all. Welcome to the land of the living, sir...' He held out a gnarled hand and Dev moved as swiftly as he could across the kitchen to take it.

'Thank you,' Dev said. The hand grasping his was stronger than he would have thought possible in one so old—firm and sure and welcoming. Maybe he wasn't as old as Dev had thought. 'And thank you very much for the clothes.' Dev hesitated, letting Joseph's words sink in. 'Did you say I was "Maggie's driftwood?"'

'There's been a big sea over the past few days.' Joseph chuckled, remembering. 'Big winds. Yesterday, Maggie said as soon as she'd done the kelp she was off to hunt for driftwood. Instead of bringing home a tree trunk or two, she brought home you.'

'I'm sorry to be a disappointment.' Dev sank thankfully into a chair on the other side of the stove. The chair felt like heaven…

'Can't be helped. We only use the driftwood as fire fuel, and Maggie says you near as heck got burned yourself.' The old eyes narrowed. 'Got yourself a fair bump or two in the process. Bad?'

'No.'

'Liar,' the old man said cheerfully. 'Still, you're young. You'll live. The little 'un was lucky.'

'Where is Dominic?' Dev asked, and it was impossible to keep the anxiety from his voice. Joseph shook his head.

'Beats me. Maggie had a bit of fun persuading him to wear one of her jogging suits, but once he realised it wasn't pink he was okay. He'll be down at the dairy, I'll be guessing—or off around the island somewhere with Lucy. I wouldn't worry. There's not much trouble a lad his age can get in around here. He seems sensible enough, and he's taken with the dog. Lucy will look after him.' His gaze intensified, fixing Dev like a bug under a microscope. 'Has he got a dog of his own?'

'No.' Dev frowned. A dog… No, he didn't think so. Gay wouldn't…

'You don't sound like you're sure.'

'He's been living with his mother...'

'One of these broken homes,' Joseph said disparagingly. 'So what's happening? His mother doesn't want him? That's the look he's got, poor little blighter. He looks like Lucy's the most dependable living thing he's seen for a while. Hungry?'

Dev blinked. There was anger building from the contempt in the old man's eyes, but he wasn't being given a chance to defend himself. And...was he hungry?

He was ravenous, he realised. Starving! He'd bought Dominic a hamburger at the airport yesterday, but Dev's stomach had been too churned up to eat, so it was twenty-four hours since he'd seen food.

'Thought so,' Joseph said in satisfaction, and Dev frowned. The old man was practically reading his mind. 'Sorry, but you'll have to get it yourself. I know you hurt, but my legs don't work so good.'

'Is this your walking stick, sir?'

'Call me Joe,' Joseph growled. 'Everyone does. Joseph's for introductions, weddings and funerals, but there's a lack of weddings these days and I'm not thinking funeral yet. And, yes, it's my walking stick, but it's not much use to me now. I've had a stroke. Maggie reckons she'll get me walking again, but I'm not so sure. She'll be in soon, and start bossing me around in some dratted walking frame thing she has, but meanwhile... Pan's on the stove, bacon's on the table, there's a couple of eggs...bread's in the cupboard. Maggie said it'll hurt but you should be able to cope. If you're hungry enough...'

He was. Dev hauled himself back to his feet and started cooking, moving minimally and gritting his teeth, but by the time he'd loaded his plate with fried eggs, bacon and fried bread, and made coffee, his leg had improved. He was moving more freely, and with less pain.

It was with relief, though, that he sat down again to demolish his meal, but no sooner had he sat than Maggie burst through the door. She stopped dead and stared—and so did Dev.

Maggie was back to how he'd first seen her. She was wearing jeans, a battered windcheater, no socks and her sneakers had one toe gone. Her hair was pulled back into a knot again, but it was doing its damnedest to escape. The snub nose and freckles made her look…

Fourteen?

'I'm twenty-nine,' she said, grinning at the look on his face and crossing to pour herself coffee from the pot Dev had put back on the stove. She sank down at the table beside him and took a mouthful. 'Wonderful. I've been hanging out for coffee for an hour. Those clothes look great on you. Khaki work gear and those bruises—you look like something out of a jungle war movie. Oh, and that was what you were going to ask, wasn't it? How old I was?'

'I might not have been so rude.' Dev stared. It was impossible not to. The lady was….magnetic?

'I'm used to being asked,' she said cheerfully. 'Sometimes I still have to show my driving licence before I can buy alcohol or get into movies. I'm sorry I wasn't here to feed you or heat water so you could wash. I could have woken you before I left but it seemed a shame. Has Grandpa looked after you?'

'He's looked after himself, girl,' Joe growled. 'Cold washing don't hurt anyone. What have you done with the little 'un?'

'He and Lucy are over at the beach.' Maggie's face clouded.

'There's nothing wrong?' Dev said quickly, and Maggie shook her head—but she didn't smile again.

'No. Just…'

'Just?'

'I can't make him laugh.'

'His mother doesn't want him,' Joe muttered, and Maggie stared—and so did Dev. These two were so darned quick…

'I didn't say that,' he protested.

'It's true, though,' Joe probed. 'Isn't it?'

'I…'

'Told you so.'

Hell!

'Why doesn't his mother want him?' Maggie asked. She peered over her coffee mug at Dev, her green eyes searching while he tried vainly to concentrate on his breakfast. Those eyes…

'Why don't you just guess?' Dev said. 'You two seem really good on guesswork.'

'It's the seaweed.' Maggie chuckled. 'It makes us omniscient—but it doesn't answer this question.'

'Look, I'm sorry, but it's none…'

'Of our business. No, but if we're to help him…'

'You don't need to help him,' Dev said heavily. He took a deep breath. He seemed to have crashed himself into these two people's lives, as well as onto their island, but enough was enough.

'You've done more than you need already,' he said at last. 'You've saved our lives and given us a place to sleep and we're more than grateful. But now… We need to get out of your lives.' And get on with ours, was the unspoken message, and Maggie's intelligent eyes showed she'd caught it. 'If I can use your telephone…?'

'Radio,' Joe told him. 'No such thing as a telephone here.'

'Radio, then,' Dev agreed. 'I'll organise a helicopter pick-up from the mainland.'

'Really?' Maggie's eyes searched his. 'How do you intend to do that?'

'I'm sure there are helicopters for hire.'

'Only two with the range that'll get them this far,' Maggie told him. 'And don't look like that. It's not second sight telling me. We know. We live here—and believe me, when you live here you get to know emergency escape routes pretty fast. If we'd asked for the air ambulance last night you would have got off the island because it was an emergency, but now... We've assured them you're okay so you'll have to join the queue.'

'Queue?'

'I was on the radio to Melbourne this morning,' Maggie told him. 'Just trying to figure things out, in case you wanted evacuation...'

'And?'

'This airline strike's downed every commercial plane in the country. Everyone's screaming for transport, the strike looks like running into next week, and the two charter helicopter services are booked flat out until then. I'm afraid, Mr Macafferty, that you should have taken the ambulance last night—because you're stuck here now, for as long as it takes.'

CHAPTER THREE

IT TOOK Dev a full hour on the radio before he accepted what Maggie had told him, and when he finally did he was horrified. A week… There was no helicopter available for love nor money.

'I'm afraid money isn't an issue,' the helicopter charter rep told him after a tortuous process of getting through. 'We could demand a hundred times what we're asking and still be frantic.'

'But I'm stuck,' Dev said blankly.

'So's everyone else, sir,' the officer said sadly. 'I'm sorry.'

There was nothing else he could do. Dev spent another half-hour trying to get messages to business colleagues and Molly and Myrtle—heaven, they'd be killing each other by now—and then went back to the kitchen to find Maggie supervising—or bossing—Joe's lesson on the walking frame.

'No luck?' she said, as he limped through the door. 'I told you so. Well, you're welcome to stay. This place has six bedrooms; there's only Grandpa and I to fill them, and it's just lucky we stocked up the freezer.'

She smiled, and it was all Dev could do not to grit his teeth. He had to be grateful, but she could sound a little less cheerful about him being trapped here!

'Don't you have a boat?' he asked, but he knew what the answer was almost before he asked. It would have to be some boat to get them to the mainland.

'Yep.' She flashed her engaging grin at him, and he knew

she was enjoying his discomfort. Why? he wondered, looking at her mischievous face. It was as if she'd decided he needed a spot of punishment... 'We sure do. It's a fishing dinghy, eight feet long and with a motor that's a bit wonky—but, hey, we have oars you can use. Or there are two canoes in the back shed if you prefer to paddle.'

Dev closed his eyes. 'Very funny!'

'We do our best,' she retorted. 'You chose to land here.'

'I need to get back to work fast.'

'That's why you didn't catch the overnight ferry to Tasmania, I guess,' she said, thinking it through aloud. 'You know, maybe it would have been more sensible to do that rather than hire a plane with a dud engine.'

'I didn't know the plane was a dud—and the ferry was booked out last night.'

'And you couldn't wait another day? I see.' Her calm eyes surveyed him, and once more he had that weird feeling that she did see—far more than he wanted—and that he was very definitely being punished.

'The ferry doesn't come anywhere near here, I suppose?' he queried. Ha! Fat chance—and Maggie's words verified it.

'You suppose right. There's no way the interstate ferry would put their passengers at risk of the reefs around here, no matter how important you are.'

'But...you have a supply boat? You must get your supplies from somewhere.'

'A boat comes in every two weeks,' Joe interjected. He'd been watching the interplay with interest. 'Came last Saturday, and it's Friday today. That's eight more nights. You're stuck here, fella. You're stuck with us, and we're stuck with you.' He shuffled forward another step on the frame and then stopped. 'I'm stuffed, Maggie. Me legs hurt. Can I sit down?'

'No. Ten minutes more, Grandpa. Twice around the kitchen—and stop complaining.'

'I can't stop here for eight days,' Dev said in dismay.

'You stop whingeing too,' she said severely, turning on him with an expression like a schoolmarm who'd just caught a particularly obnoxious student swearing. 'You should be counting your blessings. You're alive, your son's safe, and we're willing to put you up.'

'I am grateful…'

'You don't sound it.'

'I'm sitting down,' Joe said promptly. 'Maggie, shove a chair under me or I'll sit on the floor.' And, proving his point, his knees buckled and he sank backwards.

Dev reached him just in time, catching him under the shoulders. Together, he and Maggie guided the old man to his chair by the stove and Joe sank back in satisfaction. He smirked up at Maggie and folded his arms with obstinate determination.

'You haven't done enough,' Maggie said crossly.

'I can walk when I want to, but I don't want to now. I know how to walk. Go teach your grandma to suck eggs— or give Macafferty here a turn in the walking frame. He looks like he needs it.'

Maggie frowned. 'If you really won't do any more, Grandpa…'

'I won't.'

'Then I should go check on Dominic. And there's curd to press…'

'Well, quit hanging around here, girl. I've had enough of you fussing about me. Take Mr Macafferty away with you and let me be to take a nap. Make him go in the dratted walking frame.' The old man chuckled at the look on Dev's face, and his grin broadened. 'Hey, maybe his leg's too sore for the frame. I know what you ought to do. Shove him in that bath chair of mine. Then you can take him with you anywhere you want. Give him an airing…'

'Grandpa…'

'The man needs to see his son.' Joe said, humour fading as tiredness overtook him. 'And I need a sleep. Do it, Maggie. Take him away.'

'I don't think… I might just sit outside for a while,' Dev said cautiously, feeling his leg. 'Dominic will come back…'

'Not for a while he won't,' Maggie told him, frowning in concern at her grandfather and then turning her full attention on Dev, severity returning in full. She definitely disapproved—and it was definitely him she disapproved of. 'He took Lucy over to the remains of the plane. I checked on him before I came back here and he was just sitting, staring at the plane like he'd lost his world. He had his arm around Lucy, but he wouldn't speak to me. He needs you, Mr Macafferty.'

'Dev…'

'Dev, then. But there's no use making friends with me. It's your son who needs you.'

'I don't think I can…' Dev said helplessly, feeling the pain in his leg. Walking stick or not, the thought of walking to the other side of the island appalled him.

'Grandpa's right. We have a bath chair.' Maggie eyed him with a speculative gleam. She shoved her hands in her pockets and her eyes dared him. She knew, then, just how much pride was on the line here. She could guess… For him to be pushed in a bathchair… He wasn't being used to being pushed anywhere—by anyone!

'You mean you really do have a wheelchair?'

'We sure do, but Grandpa hardly needs it any more. He's getting so good in his walker—aren't you, Grandpa!'

'Go away,' Joe demanded. 'Let me sleep.'

'I'm not going in any wheelchair,' Dev retorted.

Maggie raised her mobile eyebrows, and her green eyes twinkled. 'Why not? Doesn't it suit your macho image?'

'I don't have a macho image.'

'That's fine, then, and I can't think of a single other objection you could have.' She chuckled and turned away. 'Okay, Mr Macafferty, let's find this bath chair and we'll take you for your morning constitutional. But no whinge-ing, or...'

'Or what?'

'You never know,' she said mysteriously. 'I'm a nurse, remember—and I have The Sight. Enemas at midnight spring to mind...or I might just use my seaweed and turn you into something *really* nasty!'

Which meant that she thought he was fairly nasty al-ready, Dev thought. That impression was cementing itself firmly into his mind, and he didn't like it at all.

Dev Macafferty was a man accustomed to control.

After his marriage break-up, he'd sold his cattle station, moved to Tasmania and started running eco tours—taking tourists to remote and wonderful places around the world. His company had gone from strength to strength.

As for close personal relationships? He'd lost his son—that was enough pain for one lifetime. That was the one thing that threw him out of control—the pain of emotional ties. He wasn't risking more. He *must* be in control.

But he wasn't in control now. He hadn't been in control since Gay's phone call.

And now...he was in a wheelchair surrounded by nosy goats and he was being wheeled briskly along the path leading from the house across to the beach by a woman who was treating him as if he was some sort of maw-worm.

He was totally, absolutely helpless. All he wanted to do

was put on the brakes, but the brakes were behind him, under Maggie's control. She had him right where she wanted, and there wasn't a thing he could do about it.

At least he could see. As they emerged from the house into dazzling sunlight, Dev had his first clear view of exactly where he was. The day before he'd been too dazed to take anything in.

'You live in a lighthouse!' he said on a note of discovery, shoving Ernestine's nose from his crotch.

'If you look closer, you'll see the lighthouse is separate,' she told him. 'We live in the lighthouse keeper's residence. If you look closer again you can see the lighthouse is made of stone and built to last for the next two hundred years. The house is built of rotten weather-boards and will be lucky if it makes the middle of next week. They're just a little bit different.'

Maggie spoke in the voice of one humouring a simpleton and Dev winced. Ouch.

'So…is that what you do?' he asked. 'Is that why you and your grandfather are here? As lighthouse keepers?'

'Nope.'

This was like trying to draw blood from a stone, but he wasn't to be deflected.

'Why not?'

'The light was converted to automatic ten years ago,' she said tersely. 'We just caretake the cottage and lease the land.'

Dev thought this through. The sun was warm on his face, the wind was ruffling his hair and he was being wheeled briskly along the track—and suddenly, despite his helplessness, despite Ernestine's cold nose in all the wrong places and despite Maggie's disapproval, he did feel good. What was happening might feel weird, but he was alive, and this morning he had every reason to be grateful.

'At some time in the past, Joe was the lighthouse keeper?' he probed.

'Very good,' she approved. 'Smart guess. Brains as well as beauty.'

Dev frowned, his lighter mood slipping. There was cynicism in her tone. 'Maggie…'

'Yes?'

'Am I imagining it, or am I hearing criticism?'

'Who me? Criticise?' But he was sure he was right.

'Is it because I took Dominic in an unsafe plane?'

'No…'

'We should have been safe,' he told her. 'It was hired from a reputable company. I checked its service sheets and everything seemed fine.'

'I'm sure it was.'

'Then what? What's bugging you? Why are you acting like I'm some sort of mildly retarded low-life?'

Maggie hesitated. The chair hit a bump on the path and lurched, but she appeared not to notice.

'Nothing's bugging me.'

'I'm not stupid. Tell me.'

Silence.

'Tell me!'

'Dominic tells me he's just been sent home from boarding school,' she said at last, goaded. 'He's eight years old, he seems one of the loneliest little boys I've ever met, and…*boarding school*!'

'I see.' There were echoes of Dominic's headmaster in Maggie's tone… *he's been seriously neglected*…and Dev flinched.

'Sending Dominic to boarding school wasn't my choice,' he said tersely.

'No. Of course not.' Maggie's voice said it was none of her business—but she still thoroughly, icily, disapproved.

Hell… How to explain?

'My ex-wife has… *had* custody,' Dev snapped. 'Boarding school was her decision.'

'And you're just his father, so mistakes are your wife's fault?'

'I had no say and Gay's my ex-wife. We hardly speak.'

'You wouldn't have sent him to boarding school?'

'No.'

'Then what will you do with him now?' Maggie said mildly. 'You're in a rush to get back to Tasmania. Is that because you want to spend quality time with Dominic?'

Dev paused. The woman was interrogating him as if she thought he was guilty of murder, and maybe…heck, that was how he was beginning to feel.

'I do want to spend time with Dominic,' he said ruefully. 'But…my business…I'm in the middle of urgent meetings…'

'Oh, I see.' She nodded sagely over his head and pushed his chair right at a bump. Ouch! And he was sure she'd seen it. 'And what will you do with him while you're in these meetings?' she demanded. 'Not that it's any of my business—but tell me anyway.'

'I have two aunts and a housekeeper. They'll look after him, and I'll suppose I'll find another school…' And then he glanced up and saw the deep flash of anger in her eyes, and his own anger responded. 'I won't be sending him to a boarding school,' he snapped.

'How very caring,' she said icily, and thrust the chair forward with a viciousness that was palpable. 'Two aunts and a housekeeper to care for him. How wonderful. What a dad!'

'Maggie, I have a business to run.'

'If you can afford to hire planes to cross Bass Strait and

negotiate hiring helicopters, then you can take time off to spend with your son.'

'I am. Eight days.'

'So you are,' she said cordially. 'How noble. All on your own, you've chosen to spend eight days here until the supply boat comes in. What a dad! When did you last spend time with Dominic?'

There was no answer. She'd gone too far, and his pain was far, far too deep. Dev stared straight ahead, his face wooden.

But he'd forgotten that this girl was fey. She saw... Maggie stopped the chair dead, came around the front of the wheelchair, pushed her goats out of the way and stared down at him, her face incredulous.

'You mean, you've never spent time with him?' she said slowly. 'Have you?'

'I...'

'You haven't. Why ever not?'

'His mother wouldn't let me near,' Dev said, and Maggie didn't miss the savageness in his words.

'Surely you had access?'

'Yes, but..'

'You were too busy.'

'You know nothing about it,' Dev said angrily. He shoved his hands on the wheels of the chair and pushed himself forward, so hard Maggie had to do a fast sidestep to stop him crashing into her. 'Gay blocked access at every turn.' He wheeled himself on, his anger finding an outlet in the power of the wheels, and he didn't turn to see whether she followed. 'Dominic was born after we separated and she wouldn't let me near him. And when I tried...'

He paused. The chair slowed to a halt and he put a hand to his head, which had suddenly started to ache again.

'When I tried,' he said again, and the pain in his voice was transparent, 'Dominic suffered.'

'Like how?' Maggie had stepped sideways, but now she moved back behind him, once more pushing him slowly forward through the goat herd. It made it easier somehow, to tell her when he couldn't see her. To talk of something that had hurt so much...

'Like making me out to be the big bad wolf when he was tiny.' Dev's voice was bitter beyond belief, and Maggie knew that what she was hearing had to be the truth. 'Like making me seem so bad that he'd react with fear when I went near him. By threatening to make him suffer if I demanded access, and by making me out to be the world's worst...'

'Oh, no...'

'In the end, it was easier to walk away,' Dev said wearily. 'Not easier for me, but easier...kinder for Dominic. I thought...maybe when he was older—when I could explain things—then I'd try again. But for now...he's probably scared stiff of me.'

'He's not scared stiff. Dominic's proud of you,' Maggie said softly, her eyes as warm now with sympathy as they'd been chill with condemnation before. Dev stared, caught by the warmth in her eyes and confused by her words.

'Proud...'

'When I pulled him from the plane...he said, *"My father's the same as me. His name's Devlin Macafferty, so he's D. Macafferty, too. We're the same."* A child doesn't say that about someone he fears.'

'He doesn't know me.'

'Then it's time you fixed that, and you can't do that by racing back to that very important business of yours.' She paused, then put a hand down to touch his hair. 'I'd say you've been given a very special chance, and maybe being stranded on this island wasn't only coincidence. Have you thought of that?'

'You mean Gay sabotaged the plane?' The feel of her fingers in his hair was sending shock waves right through his scalp—and somehow making the ache in his head fade to nothing. It was a gesture of a nurse to someone who was in trouble—nothing more—but it suddenly seemed more than that. Intense…intimate…

But Maggie was smiling, matching the sun with her warmth. 'Maybe I wouldn't go that far,' she told him. 'But sometimes things happen that are meant to be—and maybe spending eight days reassessing your life is just what you need.'

'You sound like my Aunty Myrtle.'

'That's my specialty,' she said, and suddenly there was a strange trace of bitterness underneath her warmth. 'I'm the world's best carer and advice giver. I can stick my oar into other people's lives, no sweat. It's just my own I stuff up.'

'Maggie…' Dev frowned, but Maggie was moving on, increasing her speed as she pushed him towards the beach.

'Come and find your son,' she said softly, swiftly, as if reminding herself to lock her shadows away again. 'The day's too fine…the sun's too warm…the wind's too fresh to be sad. It's good to be alive. Come on, Dev Macafferty, let's find your son.'

And before he could make any protest she broke into a run, and man, wheelchair and girl—and associated goats—bounded along the path to the beach with all the enthusiasm Maggie could muster.

Dominic was still sitting where Maggie had left him, on the bluff overlooking the charred remains of the plane, with Lucy sitting by his side. He looked absurdly young—almost younger than his eight years—in Maggie's jogging suit that was about four sizes too big for him.

Maggie had told Lucy to stay, and the collie was taking her responsibilities seriously. Now they both looked up, and Dominic's jaw dropped as he saw his father's method of transport.

He didn't move, though, and he didn't speak as Maggie wheeled Dev to his side.

'Hi, Dom. Hi, Luce…' Maggie squatted beside them. Dominic didn't react, but Lucy leapt into her mistress's arms and quivered her joy. 'Done anything interesting while we've been away?'

Lucy gave an excited woof. Dominic said nothing. The goats, for the moment, held back. Maybe their goat antennae were sensitive to distress, or maybe the pasture on the cliff was too delicious to pass up.

'Dominic?' Dev said gently. 'Are you okay? We were worried.'

'I'm all right. Why are you in that chair?'

'I hurt my leg.'

'Oh, yeah. I remember. Maggie showed me the bruise when I helped her off with your pants!' Unconcerned, he turned back to the plane, absorbed in its ugliness, his eyes taking in its skeletal remains.

'Do you want to come back to the house?' Maggie asked, and Dom shook his head.

'No. I'm staying here.'

'Why?' Dev asked.

'My computer's in there. Soon it'll be cold enough to have a look.'

'Dom, your computer's burned.'

'But it was in my school bag.'

'The bag won't have saved it.'

'I want to see for myself.'

'Dominic, I told you yesterday,' Dev said gently. 'I'm afraid it's destroyed, but we'll buy you another computer.'

'But when?' He choked on the beginnings of a sob. 'Maggie says we'll have to stay here for a *week,* and I have to wear her clothes. She doesn't have a computer, she doesn't have television and she doesn't have videos... she doesn't even have a real toaster! I had to have my toast cooked in a fire!'

'Hey, it was great toast,' Maggie said, offended. 'You liked it.'

'It was different!'

'It was great.'

Dominic glared, his attention diverted from his loss. 'Toast is supposed to be made in a toaster. It had black bits.'

'That's charcoal, and charcoal's good for you.'

'It is not.'

'It is so,' Maggie said, and put her hands on her hips and glared. ''Tis so, Dominic Macafferty, so there!'

'Who says?'

'Me, and I'm bigger than you. And Lucy's my dog, and if I tell her to, she'll lick you till you fall over.'

Dominic glared. He glared again and Maggie glared right back. Her eyes twinkled down at him, her chin tilted and it was too much.

Dominic gave a reluctant chuckle while Dev watched on in stunned amazement. This woman was crazy.

'You're nutty,' Dom pronounced, and Dev could only agree—and Maggie nodded.

'Yep... And you and your dad are stuck with me for a week. Toast and charcoal for a week, and a nutty me... I don't know how you'll be able to stand it.'

'I just want my computer...'

The distress returned and Dev frowned. This wasn't a

spoiled child bewailing the loss of an expensive toy. It was more than that.

'You said you won it?' he said softly, and Dominic nodded. He turned again to look sadly down at the still smouldering ruins.

'I sent in zillions of soft drink tops. Zillions and zillions, into this competition, and I won, and they sent me a computer in its own box. I even had to sign for it, and Gay said Greg already had one, so I could use it all by myself.'

'You probably have lots of other toys,' Maggie said, frowning, but Dominic shook his head fiercely.

'No. Greg's kids take them off me—they're bigger than me—but I got this the day they sent me to boarding school, and Greg was away so Greg's kids don't even know I have it.'

'Greg?' Maggie queried.

'My ex-wife's present husband,' Dev said heavily. 'She goes though husbands at a rate of knots.'

'I see.' Maggie's eyes softened in sympathy. She sank down onto the sand beside Dominic and looked down at the smouldering ruins of the plane. 'Well, Greg's kids aren't on this island,' she said softly. 'No one is, except me and my grandpa and your dad. You can play with anything you like. No one's going to stop you.'

'There's nothing to play with.'

'Try throwing a ball to Lucy and then tell me that—and anyway, who needs toys? There are better things to play with on this island than toys.'

'Like what?'

'Well, for a start there are caves. Want to see one?'

Dominic's interest was caught. He turned to face her, brushing his curls out of his eyes so he could see her better. He was *so* like his father... 'What sort of caves?' he asked.

'Pirate caves—just made for smuggling. There's one at

the end of this beach. I'll show you.' She jumped to her feet and held out her hand for him to join her. Dom looked tentatively at it—and then put his fingers into her palm like someone who had just committed himself to something he might regret.

He wasn't given time to regret anything. 'Grab the other side of your father's chair,' Maggie ordered. 'We'll have to drag him backwards across the sand.'

'Hey, I'm not being dragged anywhere...' Dev said, startled.

'Shut up, you—this is our adventure,' Dev was told kindly. 'Dominic, your dad can be our captive, chained to his chair, about to be interred in our deepest, darkest dungeon for thirty days and thirty nights...'

Dev stared. The change on Dominic's face was stunning. The bleak look had disappeared entirely. He looked bemused, absorbed and totally fascinated. Then, before Dev could comment, Maggie had spun his chair around so he was facing away from the sea.

'Okay, Dominic,' she ordered, placing his small hand on the opposite chair handle to hers. 'Pull. Let's get this pirate captive right where he belongs.'

And the next minute Dev was being hauled backwards across the beach by two very determined persons, and he had no say in the matter at all.

He was so far out of control he was practically in orbit.

It took ten minutes of heavy haulage before they did it. Dev was all for getting out of the chair and helping, but whenever he suggested it Maggie's two hands came down on his shoulders and he was put firmly back in his place.

'Sit,' she said, in the same tone she used with Lucy. 'You're our captive. You do as we say and nothing else.'

So Dev submitted, sitting and wondering just what the heck was going on.

He'd had more comfortable rides in his time—in fact, riding an unbroken horse back in his farming days sprang to mind as a more comfortable alternative. Dom and Maggie tilted the chair and hauled it backwards along the sand, but their different heights and strengths made the going rough.

A couple of times Dev lurched so far sideways he thought he was gone, but each time Maggie managed to bounce around to Dom's side of the chair in time to right it. She was like a jack rabbit, he thought dazedly. A nutty, lovely, laughing jackrabbit…

Finally they reached the end of the beach, where a slab of flat rock reached out over the sand to mark the entrance to a cave beyond. Dev sighed in relief as the wheels of his chair hit level ground.

'Great,' Maggie said in satisfaction. 'That's the hard bit done. Now we can run…' And she hauled her side faster. With a gasp of delight, Dominic lurched after her…and so did the chair…and Dev…

And Lucy…

And the goats, for heaven's sake… As they made it to the mouth of the cave, Ernestine looked curiously along the beach from where she was grazing—and broke into a gallop as she saw something so interesting on her patch. The herd followed. Dev looked back at them—there was nothing else he could do but look backwards and try to stay in his bouncing chair—and his weirdness intensified. Stuck in a wheelchair, being hauled into pirate caves, being chased by goats…

He was supposed to be in a company board meeting right at this minute, he told himself helplessly, and wondered suddenly what his fellow board members would say if they could see him now... Dev Macafferty, head of Macafferty Eco Tours, stuck in a wheelchair being chased by goats...

Despite himself, Dev felt the sides of his mouth twitch into a grin. For heaven's sake...

And then they were in the cave. The cave was vast and deep and scary, with the echoes of the surf outside resounding around and around, booming along the walls and hammering into their heads.

Maggie hauled the chair back so they were just out of the light—where the gloom of the cave was almost overwhelming. Then she spun his chair around so he was facing the entrance and left him, abandoning Dev and taking Dominic's hand.

'There. We have our prisoner safe. No one will find him now!'

Wrong...

Thirty silhouettes appeared against the light, and thirty shadows edged forward...

'Yikes,' Dominic said in mock alarm, and Dev stared at the sound of delight in the small boy's voice. His tone echoed Maggie's. 'It's the cavalry.'

'They're on our side,' Maggie assured him.

'How do we know?' Dom asked, fascinated.

'They didn't say a password.' Her voice was now grave as a judge. 'You didn't hear them say a password?'

'N...no...'

'There you are, then,' she said smugly. 'Enemies always say passwords. They expect it, you see, so I've taught my troops to give passwords a miss. I've trained them to be silent as the grave—except for the odd bleat or two.'

'You're joking.' In the dim light, Dominic's face was half-laughing, half-deadly serious, and Dev grinned to see it.

'Nope. You try giving them a secret message and see

what they do with it,' Maggie assured him. 'They do what all good cavalrymen have been trained to do for thousands of years. They memorise every word—and then they eat the message.'

It was too much. His reserve gone, Dominic chuckled, and released Maggie's hand. He took a couple of tentative steps forward, Ernestine Goat, the leader of the pack, took a couple of steps forward herself, and suddenly Dominic was surrounded by goats, each one trying her best to sniff this strange new person on their island.

Maggie made to step forward as well, but Dev's hand shot out to grasp hers, holding her at his side.

'Maggie…'

She looked a query down at him. 'Yes?'

'Maggie, this is wonderful.'

'You like my cave?' She looked down at their linked hands, as if expecting him to release her, but he did no such thing.

'No. You.'

'I beg…?'

'I meant, you're wonderful,' he said too quickly, and then hesitated. What was it about this woman that had him on the wrong foot? He was usually self-assured—confident—completely at home with women. Now he felt like some sort of stupid schoolboy.

Get hold of yourself, Macafferty…

'I just meant that what you're doing for Dominic is great,' he said softly. 'You don't know it, but Dominic was in that damned boarding school for three months, and in that time the headmaster never saw him smile. That was why they asked that he leave. He hasn't smiled for so long—and yet, in one short day….'

'You're saying we've hit on a smile formula?' Maggie grinned herself, but she shook her head, her curls bouncing free. Her ribbon had given up the ghost somewhere across the island; her hair ran riot and it suited her wild... 'It'll never sell,' she said. 'Nearly kill a child in an aeroplane, burn his computer and stick his dad in a wheelchair... Sure, I agree, it's enough to make anyone smile, but I defy you to bottle it as a cure-all.' She looked down at him—and her smile faded.

Slowly she hauled her hand back—but Dev didn't release it. There was tension growing between them that he couldn't figure out. It was as if there was some sort of link, and he very much didn't want the link to be broken.

'Saleable formula or not, you've made him smile,' he said softly. 'I'm incredibly grateful.'

'That's good.' She hesitated, and the tension mounted even more. Maggie looked down at their linked hands. Her fingers moved within his and the link strengthened.

It couldn't last. It was crazy—stupid—and Maggie was a sensible, logical woman. Not crazy in the least. He could see that.

'Can I have my hand back, please?' she asked, in a voice that wasn't quite steady, and finally Dev nodded. He released her hand and let it fall—and as it slipped away he noticed the gleam of gold on the third finger.

A wedding ring?

'You're married?' he asked, and he heard Maggie's sharp intake of breath over the sound of the waves echoing around the cave.

'N...no.'

'You wear a wedding ring.'

'So I do.'

'Why?'

She chewed her bottom lip—and then she shrugged.

'That, Dev Macafferty,' she said softly, 'is none of your

business. You're a captive on my island—and good captives know their place.'

'Which is butting out of your personal life?'

'Ernestine is the only one around here allowed to butt anywhere,' she told him. 'Speaking of which…' She managed a chuckle. 'The goats have finished their inspection of Dominic, and I think we should get out of here while the going's good.'

'You mean the tide might come in?'

'Nothing so wholesome.' She grinned. 'You have thirty goats in a confined space between you and the entrance to the cave,' she said. 'And my goats produce the sweetest smelling cheese and the foulest smelling manure in all the land. Even now, Mr Macafferty, you're risking major trauma setting your wheelchair wheels toward the entrance. However…if you'd like to stay and chat some more…'

'Get me out of here,' he said with feeling.

'You know, I thought that's what you might say.'

Maggie grabbed his wheelchair and pushed him forward so fast it was as if she was afraid—and Dev knew suddenly it wasn't just the smell of goats this lady was afraid of.

There was something between them that he didn't understand at all.

CHAPTER FOUR

AFTER the cave, they made their way to the other side of the island to the dairy. It was tough pushing Dev's chair, but he still wasn't permitted to get out of it, and Dom seemed to enjoy the novelty of shoving a parent around. So Dev sat, feeling guilty but submissive, and let himself be taken where they willed.

'Don't quibble,' Maggie told him. 'I need to go to the dairy, so you're coming too. There's work to do, even if you guys are in holiday mode.'

The dairy... Work...

Dev looked about him as they crossed the rocky island paths, expecting any minute to see a cow or two, but there was nothing but goats.

And there *was* nothing but goats. The dairy was a cow shed in miniature.

'The dairy's for goats?' Dev said in amazement, as Maggie pushed him inside. And then he stared some more. The rest of the island—including Maggie herself—looked as if it was caught in a time warp somewhere in the middle of last century, but not the dairy. There were stainless steel milk vats, polished until you could see your face in them, a spotless concrete floor and whitewashed walls, huge refrigerators, and the low hum of a generator making the first unnatural noise Dev had heard on the island.

'Why wouldn't I milk goats?' she asked.

But it was Dominic who spoke next, his eyes widening. His quick young mind had worked at a tangent.

59

'Was that goat milk I drank for breakfast?' he demanded, his voice appalled, and Maggie grinned.

'Yep. It sure was. You drank goat's milk and you ate charcoal toast made on a fire. It's a wonder you're still alive!'

'Oh, yuk!'

'You say that to Ernestine,' Maggie warned. 'She'll be so offended you'll be butted off the island.'

'But…' While Dom clutched his stomach in imaginary poison mode, and Maggie laughed, Dev was thinking things through. He stared around at the set-up, both in the milking shed and through the door into what looked like some sort of processing room. 'Goat cheese…' he said slowly. 'Back in the cave you said your goats make the sweetest cheese… How much milk does one goat give a day?'

'Over a litre.'

'You have thirty goats?'

'Yep.'

'So you're milking thirty litres a day?'

'Forty. Or more.'

'Don't quibble.'

'I'm not quibbling.'

'So how much cheese do you and your grandfather eat?'

She chuckled then. 'Not so much as that. It's good cheese, but there are limits to everything. Okay, you want to see my operation?'

'Very much.' Dev was intrigued, and so was Dominic. With the instant recovery of the very young, he'd now forgotten he was fatally poisoned, and was staring at the milking machines in fascination.

'Maggie, do you put these cup things on their…on their…?' he asked.

'"Teats" is the polite word.' Maggie opened a cupboard and produced three pairs of white gum boots. 'Yep. I put the cups on their teats, and they're milked by the machine. If I was tough as old boots I'd milk them by hand—but I'm not. You can help me tonight if you like. It'll take your mind off missing your computer.'

'Me? Put things on their…teats?'

'Yep. Put some boots on.' Then she looked dubiously at Dev. 'Can you stand, do you think? I don't think I can put the chair through the sanitary solution.'

'What's that?' Dom was practically pop-eyed as Maggie motioned to a shallow trough of what looked like water.

'Disinfectant. You need to stand in that going into the cheese room, and then again coming out. It keeps bugs out of our cheeses. Oh, and you have wear these neat little hats.'

'Why?'

'Because I don't like hair in my cheese. Mr Macafferty, if you lean on me, would you like to come in and see my cheese?'

There was no stopping him. Like Dominic, he was agog.

The cheese processing plant was so efficient that Dev could only marvel. He stood back while Dominic washed his hands cleaner than he thought any small boy had washed his hands in living memory, then dipped his arms elbow-deep into a tub of warm, slimy curds. As Maggie said, 'just to feel'.

And… 'It feels great,' Dom announced, breathless with wonder and holding up a vast chunk of curd for Dev to see. 'Really slimy and disgusting. And it's warm. It's even better than Slurpo. Put your hands in, Dad, and get a handful.'

Dad…

Dominic had never referred to Dev as Dad before. No one had ever referred to Dev as Dad, and Dev looked at

Dominic's intense, excited face and felt his heart twist. Dad...

'What's Slurpo?' Maggie said faintly, giving Dev a sideways curious glance, and Dominic grinned. If the little boy wasn't careful he might just get used to grinning, Dev thought dazedly. Dom had smiled at least three times now. And he'd called him...

Dad?

'The kids have Slurpo at school. It comes in tubs and it's green,' Dom told them, failing to notice the strange way his father was looking at him—or the way Maggie was looking at his dad. 'If you chuck it at the ceiling before a teacher comes, then it sticks for about five minutes—and then drops on some kid. Or even on the teacher! Gay and Greg wouldn't buy me any, so I just had to watch the other kids, but this is better.'

He was into everything, and Maggie put him to work lifting the curd out of the warm whey and into the cheesecloth.

In comparison, Dev hardly noticed the cheesemaking process. He was too busy watching Maggie and his son.

'Now it has to drain,' Maggie announced, sending another odd glance at Dev.

Yeah, right, he thought. She was fey. She'd be guessing exactly what he was thinking—that he was so choked up it was all he could do not to burst into tears.

But she didn't comment. Wisely, she kept the conversation practical.

'Tomorrow we put it into brine, and the next day we drain it again, cut it and pack it into jars, with oil, herbs and garlic,' she told them. 'Then it's stored to wait for the next boat to the mainland.'

Dev was limping around the processing room, looking as if he was examining everything while really he was just watching his son—and watching Maggie of the green eyes and the gorgeous chuckle—but now he lifted a pile of labels and made a discovery.

'You're Windswept Cheeses!'

Maggie shook her head in mock wonder. 'You can read! I knew you were clever...'

'But I buy this cheese!' Dev said slowly. 'It's wonderful. The food critics go into raptures over it. It's as hard to find as hen's teeth, but it's great.'

'If you can afford to buy it, then you must have more money than I do.'

'He has,' Dominic announced, carefully arranging his lumps of curd onto cloth. 'Gay says the only good thing about Dad is that he's rich.'

'Gee, thanks...' Dev said faintly.

'It's true,' Dom told him. 'Before she married Greg, Gay said if she knew you were going to end up loaded then she'd have stayed married to you.'

Now there was a thought... Marriage to Gay again? Heaven forbid. In fact, marriage at all? No way.

Or maybe that was what he'd thought until he'd met this amazing Maggie, Dev thought suddenly, as his mind took a crazy sideways step. Horizons were opening up all over the place, in the face of his stunned reaction to this woman.

But Maggie hardly seemed to be listening. Dev's riches were nothing to do with her. She placed more cloth on the top of Dom's curd, weighted it and then turned back to them. 'Okay, we can go now,' she told them. 'That's all I need to do for the moment.'

'You must be doing okay if you're Windswept Cheeses,' Dev said, forcing his mind back to cheese, but Maggie shook her head.

'We break even. The income from the kelp means we can update the dairy a bit—but we live on the smell of an oily rag. Yes, we charge a fortune for our cheese, but we can't increase our herd. Extra goats on the island would destroy the grasses that give our cheese such a distinctive taste. And the costs of living here...the transport...'

'And it must be darned hard work,' Dev said reflectively. 'Milking thirty goats...making cheese and collecting your kelp...'

'It's what I choose.'

'Is it?' His eyes narrowed. There were things here that didn't add up—that he didn't understand. Maggie's nursing background...the wedding ring on her left hand...

And there were shadows. Maggie moved in a constant bubble of laughter, but he didn't have to look very deep to see shadows behind the joy.

What had she given up to come here?

'Okay, back to the house for lunch,' she said firmly, as if guessing he was about to open his mouth and ask questions. 'It's soup and bread and...guess what? Cheese! Then a rest for you, Dev Macafferty, because that leg has done enough for one morning, and a rest for you as well, Dominic, if you like, but Lucy and I need to collect kelp.'

'I'm not resting. I'm coming with you, kelp collecting,' Dominic said eagerly—and it was all Dev could do not to say the same.

This lady had mystery written all over her, he thought, and it was starting to become increasingly—strangely—important to find out just what that mystery was.

Not that it had anything to do with him, he told himself hastily. It didn't matter.

It was just...he badly wanted to know.

After lunch, Maggie ordered Dev to his bedroom, and he was grateful to submit. He was asleep two minutes later, and he didn't wake until after dark. When he did, he flexed his leg and it felt infinitely better.

The room was in darkness, lightened only by the faint glimmer of moonlight from the window. His window faced away from the lighthouse, there were no street lamps here, nor were there rumblings of distant traffic. This island had to be one of the most isolated places on earth.

So what was Maggie doing here?

For heaven's sake, what was he doing thinking straight away of Maggie? He was going nuts. Women didn't affect him like this—did they?

This one did!

Fumbling on the bedside table, he found matches and lit his candle, then checked his watch. Eight-thirty…

He must have missed dinner.

His stomach was making up for lost ground. He'd eaten a substantial lunch, but now he very definitely wanted more. Maybe the whole household had gone to bed, he thought, but he could get himself to the kitchen and find some of Maggie's glorious cheese…

And maybe find Maggie…

Stop it, Macafferty. Think about Dominic. Think about food.

Think about Maggie…

It was as he'd hoped. Maggie was in the kitchen. The kitchen door was open, there was no light, but the door of the fire stove was pushed wide and she was sitting watching the flame inside. The ever-present sound of the sea masked the sound of his coming, so she didn't look up.

Dev's insides gave a strange little kick when he saw her. She hadn't heard him, and by the look on her face she was a long, long way away from here.

He wasn't wrong about her shadows, he thought as he

watched her. Maggie was back in her homespun skirt again. Her face was leaning towards the fire, with the light from the flames flickering over her finely boned features, her eyes were framed by her riot of hair—and it was as if she was trying to draw warmth from the flames.

Not warmth, he saw suddenly. Comfort.

It had to be something bad, he thought—to make her look like that.

'Maggie?' Dev's voice was soft, but she jumped, startled out of her reverie. The shadows disappeared at once—the transformation was so fast he could almost have imagined them—and her lovely smile flooded her face again.

'Well, if it isn't sleepyhead…'

But he couldn't ignore the look of pain he'd caught. He was sure he wasn't imagining it. 'Maggie, what's wrong?'

'Nothing's wrong.' She stood and pressed her hands to her face in a gesture of control—pulling herself back together—and the moment was lost. Whatever it was, he wouldn't hear of it now. 'How are you?'

'I'm fine, but you…' He limped forward, and would have taken her hands, but she slipped sideways to put the table between them.

'We saved some dinner for you. I'll get you a plate. You must be hungry.'

Dev frowned, watching her eyes, but he decided finally to let it go. 'Has Dominic gone to bed?'

'Yes.' She smiled again, and the shadows retreated further. 'He's had a lovely afternoon—he's been so busy he's even admitted he hasn't missed his computer. I brought him in to say goodnight, but you didn't wake, and he slept the minute his head hit the pillow.'

'That's terrific.' Heaven, how restful her voice was. She moved around the kitchen with the grace of someone from the spirit world. Not just fey…unworldly.

'I don't know why I slept.' For some reason his voice wouldn't work the way it should. There was something about Maggie that splintered his usual confidence and had him feeling like a schoolboy—or one of her patients. That was how she treated him, he thought ruefully—how she thought of him—and he wasn't accustomed to women thinking of him as an incidental being.

She didn't seem to be noticing his discomfort. 'It wasn't a minor accident you had yesterday,' she told him softly, gentle sympathy in her lovely voice. 'You nearly died, and knocking yourself out like that... It'll be the head injury, plus shock making you sleep. And also...' She looked across the darkened room at him, then smiled. She lit the lantern in the middle of the table, as if she'd only just realised it was almost dark, and then looked at him more closely. 'I'm guessing you were tired before the accident. Dominic tells me you work very hard.'

'Dom tells you...' Dev stared. 'Dom doesn't know anything about me.'

'He certainly does.'

'He can't. He hasn't been allowed near me. I've written to him, of course, and sent birthday and Christmas gifts. But Gay sends back everything unopened.'

'Well, letters or not, he still knows,' Maggie said definitely. 'When I put him to bed tonight he told me all about your business, and he gave me a list of every country where you run tours. He has them off pat in his head—memorised—and that's no mean feat. You run an extensive outfit.'

'I...yes,' Dev said blankly, trying to take this on board. Dominic knew... 'Gay must have told him about it,' he said slowly. It didn't seem like Gay—but, once more, Maggie was way ahead of him.

'He hasn't heard about you from his mother,' she told him. 'He reads the advertisements for your company's tours in the newspapers. He says he searches for your ads in every newspaper he can get his hands on, and he makes lists. You might not know much about him, but he's a walking encyclopedia for Macafferty tours.'

Dev stared. He sat down heavily at the table as Maggie served out a plateful of casserole—a curry, which smelled just wonderful—and finally took this in.

'But...why?'

'I think he's been hungry for a father for a very long time,' Maggie said gently. 'I think you have a son just waiting to be taken into your heart, and he's a lovely little boy, aching to be loved. All you need to give him is time.'

'I won't rush him.'

'I don't mean that. I mean...give him *your* time. Give part of you.' She shook her head at his blank look. 'It's not going to be easy, is it? You've been independent for so long.'

'I guess...' But it was true. He had been independent. And Dev's mind had been working this problem over and over since the moment of Gay's phone call. How to fit Dominic around his frantic business affairs...?

'Dev, it's not a matter of fitting Dominic into your life,' Maggie said, guessing once more where his thoughts were taking him. 'It's a matter of fitting your life around Dominic's. I don't care how much money you have—Dominic is the most important thing in your life right now, and I hope you realise it.'

'I do.'

She smiled, bestowing her gracious approval, and once more Dev had the overwhelming impression she thought he was some sort of emotional half-wit—needing to be given lessons in loving his son...

Maybe she was right at that.

He sat and ate his casserole—and, miraculously, drank a couple of glasses of really good red wine—while Maggie watched with the aura of a benevolent genie. Afterwards she poured him coffee and watched him drink that, then rose and took his plates to the sink.

He rose as well, edging her firmly aside to take the dish-cloth away from her.

'There's no need for you...'

'To wash dishes,' he finished for her. 'Yes, there is. I'm fine, my leg feels a hundred per cent, my head's not aching—so don't be a doormat, Maggie.'

'I'm no doormat.'

'What time do you milk your goats in the morning?'

'First light.'

'About five-thirty? Great. You should be in bed right now.'

'If I go to bed this early I don't sleep.'

Dev nodded, started the tap and turned to lift the kettle across so he could wash with warm water. 'So you don't sleep well. You know, I suspected that. What's worrying you?'

She stopped reaching back for her dishcloth, and she stared. 'Hey, I'm supposed to be the one with second sight,' she said, trying to keep it light, but her voice was shaken. 'Have you been eating my seaweed?'

'I don't need seaweed to see what's obvious. There are shadows under your eyes.'

'So I use eyeshadow.'

'Very fetching. What's the shade? Dead Beat, or Worried Sick—or Pain-In-The-Past?'

'N...nothing.'

'Liar.'

'Hey, I don't need an inquisition,' she said, flashing anger. 'If you're helping with the washing up, then wash, and leave me alone.'

'You won't tell me?'

'No. It's none of your business.'

'But…there is something upsetting you.'

'Dev, leave it,' she said distressfully. 'I haven't come all the way to Grandpa's island to be met with interrogation by complete strangers.'

'You're running away?'

'Yes. No! I came here because my grandmother died and Grandpa had a stroke. He needs me.'

'So what would have happened if you hadn't come?'

'Grandpa would have gone into a nursing home on the mainland. He'd be miserable, and I won't have that.'

'But…before he had his stroke…' Dev concentrated on scrubbing the casserole pan for a moment while he thought things through. It needed concentration. The bottom of the pan was burned black. 'Before your grandmother died…I assume you were living somewhere else?'

'Yes, but…'

'Wouldn't it have been easier to take Joe to the mainland to live with you?'

'I told you—he'd have been miserable.'

'Not necessarily.' She definitely wasn't the only one who could read minds, Dev thought, watching her face. There was more to this than Joe's wish to stay on the island.

But Maggie wasn't having any nosiness. 'How do you know?' she demanded crossly. 'Of course he would have been miserable.'

'I don't know for sure,' Dev admitted, scrubbing harder. Good grief, something really stubborn had been incinerated in the bottom of this pan. It was clinging as if it was glued. 'Sure, he wouldn't be as happy as he was here when he was well—but he's restricted in his movements now, and if he had his dog and a good fire and someone to talk to at night…'

'He's not restricted,' she said angrily. 'Or he won't be. He'll be up walking again.'

'He's tired, Maggie. He's very old. Joe wants to be left to sit. Sure, he needs exercise, but I can't see him bounding over the island again—milking the goats—gathering kelp—can you?'

'I…'

'Will you do that for him until he dies?'

'Yes! If I need to.'

'If he needs it—or if you need it?'

'Dev…' Her eyes flashed anger, but there was distress behind them. She picked up a plate and wiped it dry, put it down, and then picked it up again. She stared at it sightlessly, then put it back. Dev left his pan, turned and took both her hands in his. He hadn't been wrong. She was in trouble.

'Maggie…'

His touch made her gasp. 'Go back to your washing up,' she said, hauling back and trying for lightness. 'Men always try to get out of the dishes.'

'I already told you I'll do them all.'

'They always say that, too. ''Leave them to me,'' they say, but when you wake up in the morning you find they're still soaking.'

'This casserole dish doesn't just need soaking. It needs dynamite. You cooked something in here that's getting its own back, vengeance wise.'

'It was your fault I had to keep it hot for so long—so get back to scrubbing and let go of my hands.' She glowered and pulled, then pulled harder.

'Yes, ma'am.' He could take a hint. He released her and backed off a bit, and thought that maybe touching her had been a mistake. The tension between them was building by the minute, and he didn't know how to handle it.

Neither did she. One look at her face told him she was as confused as he was.

There was silence; the silence grew, and something else grew with it. It was unsubstantial—nothing—yet it was so real Dev could almost reach out and touch it. It was an emotional pull between them that was threatening to take over, and Maggie's eyes showed she didn't know what on earth to do.

'If…if you're offering to finish here then I'll go outside for a walk,' she managed finally, trying to drag her eyes from his and failing.

A walk. Now that was an idea.

'Me too.'

'You have a sore leg.'

'It's better.'

'How can it be better already? This morning you were in a wheelchair.'

'The wheelchair wasn't my idea.'

'You were glad enough to sit in it.' The tension between them wasn't decreasing one bit. They were talking through it—over it—but it was still there. 'Anyway, I'm going up into the lighthouse,' Maggie said firmly. 'I always do this time of night to…to check. I took Dominic there earlier, but you…with that leg there's no way you can climb.'

'Try me.'

'Oh, for heaven's sake…' Maggie took a deep breath. 'Don't be ridiculous.'

'You can climb to the top of the lighthouse?' he demanded.

'Yes. There are stairs and we have a key, but…'

'You're saying we could go up to the top of the lighthouse while we wait for the remnants of this casserole to release their fearsome grip?'

She tried to smile. 'I…no. I didn't say that. Your leg…'

'There's a handrail up the stairs?'

'Yes, but…'

'I'll haul myself up.' He looked down at her in the dim light, certainty fading. 'Maggie, I'm not sure what's happening here,' he told her. 'I've been asleep for too long. My head feels like it's full of cotton wool and I badly need to clear it.'

'I shouldn't have given you red wine.'

'Yes, you should. You very definitely should. It's made my leg feel a whole heap better.'

'It's not up to climbing stairs.' She was back to being snappy, defensive as a hedgehog.

'The way I'm feeling, I reckon I could sit on my backside and haul myself up,' he told her. The need to get out of this kitchen—to get some distance between him and Maggie and to figure out just what was going on between them was almost overwhelming. Or maybe…just to climb a lighthouse with her…

'Come on, Maggie,' he told her. 'We can check Dominic is asleep and then leave this casserole dish to self-detonate—or hope it does. It's as useful as anything I'm doing with a scrubber. Take me and show me Listall Island by night.'

'Dev… Honestly, your leg… I don't want to hurt you,' she faltered, and he shook his head.

'You won't hurt me, Maggie. I don't think you could ever hurt me. I don't think you'd know how.'

The lighthouse was fifty yards from the cottage, perched on the highest part of the island. From the base it looked almost eerie, a vast column of white stone towering over its rocky base. Dev reached the base and hesitated, leaning heavily on his walking stick. His leg was improving by the minute, but he didn't want to push it by going too fast.

'It looks haunted,' he said, looking up.

Maggie looked at him, considering, the tension still there. When she spoke, the humour was forced. 'Are eco tour operators scared of ghosts?'

'Definitely.'

She managed a grin. 'Then it's definitely haunted.'

Dev gave a deep breath. He reached forward to take the key Maggie carried, unlocked the lighthouse door and gave Maggie a gentle push inside.

'After you, then,' he said. 'I'm right behind you.'

'Your leg's not up to it.'

'If it hurts, I'll stop.'

'You…' She took a deep breath. 'You don't want to hold my arm up the stairs?'

He did—very much—and not because he needed her support. But the tension was still heavily between them and taking her arm wasn't any way to alleviate that.

'Nope. You go and meet your boogies first. Warn them I'm coming and tell them I'm friendly.'

'I'll tell them you're nuts.' She smiled. 'Your leg will hurt like blazes, and it'll serve you right.'

Maybe it did hurt, but it was worth it, and it didn't kill him. Part of Dev's early life had been breaking horses, which had meant kicks and falls, and this seemed no worse. He used the handrail to help him up the spiral staircase, putting most of the weight on his arms, and he managed better than he'd thought he would.

Maggie didn't carry a torch, and she didn't need one—there were slits built into the stone walls at regular intervals, letting the moonlight flicker through to light their way. Maggie's long skirt swept the staircase before him, and

Dev's sense of unreality deepened. There was no need of boogies, Dev thought ruefully, as he followed her upward. He had his very own spirit lady leading him on.

At the top of the stairs there was another door and Maggie paused before opening it.

'How's the leg?'

'Fine. What are we waiting for?'

For answer she put her finger to her lips. 'Shh. This is where the boogies are.'

Dev promptly reached forward and took her hand firmly in his. She looked down at their entwined fingers, her eyes a question.

'I'm holding on in case you get frightened,' he told her.

'You mean, in case *you* get frightened,' she retorted.

'Ha! What a thought!' But he didn't let go.

No boogies leaped to meet them, but Dev didn't release her as they walked into the light chamber, and, for whatever reason, Maggie didn't pull away. He must need support, she thought to herself—so she didn't attempt to pull back. In truth, she didn't want to, and the reasons she didn't were too complex to even think about.

The link between them…the tension…was growing stronger by the minute.

The chamber's centre was taken up by a vast light, with only room for one person to stand between wall and light— or two squashed side by side, as Maggie and Dev were. The brilliant lantern above their head was surrounded by a wall of mirrors. Every twenty seconds, a beam of green light swung out, piercing the darkness of the night beyond.

It was a weird place—a place where one might reasonably expect ghosts. Anything was possible in a place like this. Dev had scarcely taken it all in when Maggie gave a silent tug on Dev's hand and motioned towards a door on the other side of the light.

'What's this?' he asked in a voice filled with foreboding. 'Lover's leap? Are there boogies out there, waiting to push us off?'

'Coward,' Maggie mocked him. 'I'm game if you're not.' And she deliberately released her fingers and walked through the door, as if unconcerned whether he'd follow or not.

He followed. Of course he followed—to the railing that ran outside the lighthouse. Here, there was much more room, and where a woman like Maggie led, a man would be crazy not to follow.

He'd follow her anywhere…

Outside, the magnificence of the view almost took his breath away.

The night was still, and the near full moon cast a silver trail across the rolling breakers of the sea below. Above their heads, the vast lighthouse lamp stretched out its warning, as if it were reaching for the trail of moonlight—seeking to touch its silver thread.

Far below, the little cottage looked even more insignificant than it did in daylight—a tiny, man-made thing, waiting to be swept away by the elements. Maggie stared down at it, and Dev watched her face…

This was so lovely. She was so lovely…

The link was hauling him in. He was captured on the strongest of lines…

'Now, I'm not showing you this so we can be included in your eco tours,' she said softly, striving for lightness. 'I want no tourists…'

'If any tourist came near this place I'd put Ernestine onto them,' Dev said simply. 'Maggie…'

'What?' She was trying to sound stern, but it didn't come off. Instead it came out sounding breathless—unsure…

But Dev was suddenly sure enough for both of them—sure of what he wanted.

'I think I want to kiss you,' he said, and he'd hardly known he was going to say the words—he'd hardly known he was going to *think* them—but he certainly had and he certainly did!

That made her even more breathless. 'I can't... Dev, I can't think why you'd want to do such a thing.'

'Can't you? You don't want to be kissed?'

'N...no.'

'You don't sound sure.'

'I...'

'You wouldn't like to just try...to see if it's as good as I think it could be?'

'Dev...'

Her eyes said it all. They were confused, bewildered—but warm and wondering, lifted to his in mute appeal. A man would have to be inhuman to resist eyes like that...

And Dev wasn't inhuman. He was under her spell. She was fey, a witch—a wonderful spirit woman—and he was the luckiest man in the world to be able to touch her.

'Maggie...'

That was all. There was suddenly nothing more to be said. Slowly, as if he was afraid she'd turn to mist under his hands, he took her into his arms.

She didn't pull back.

It was enough. Her presence...her touch was too much for any man to resist. She was far, far too lovely.

He bent his head and kissed her

And as for Maggie...

For a moment she was absolutely still—absolutely passive. *No!* her mind was screaming at her. No! You know what this does. How can you be such a fool?

But it was too late. It had been too late since the moment

she'd seen this man, she thought helplessly as his mouth claimed hers. She'd been wanting this ever since she'd first set eyes on him. The warmth of his eyes... The deep caring... The way he looked at his small son...

It was the way he looked at her, she admitted at last. Dear heaven, she wanted to feel him...wanted to touch...

And it was just how she'd imagined it could be. His mouth was on her lips and the sweetness of the kiss was so poignant she wanted to cry out with joy. It was so right. Gently her lips parted—welcoming—wanting the feel of this man against her.

He felt her give, and for a moment—a fraction of a second—Dev drew back, his eyes searching hers, as if seeking an answer for some unspoken question. What he saw must have satisfied him. With a groan, he gathered her to him, and his mouth once again found its home.

She was lost. The feel of this man against her was all that mattered. The texture of his sweater, the roughness of his unshaven skin, the hardness of his arms and the gentle exploration of his mouth were the only things in the universe.

His kiss grew deeper, his hands pulling her body further into his, demanding a response. Beyond, the light shimmered on an empty sea. They were alone, and yet if there had been a thousand spectators it would have made no difference. There was only the feel of their mouths against each other.

There was only each other. Man and woman. One.

Finally...how much longer she could never later tell... they drew apart, then stood, linked by their arms and by their need, but each shaken and unsure.

'Maggie?' Dev's voice held a tremor she hadn't heard before. Had he felt it too, then? This shaking of their universe? This shifting of their very foundations?

'Dev.' Her voice was a husky whisper. What was this man doing to her? She should break and run, yet his eyes held hers, infinitely tender, warm and strong, locking her to him as surely as the strongest chain. For the life of her, she couldn't move.

'Maggie…you're so lovely.'

'It's the light,' she managed, somehow finding the strength to chuckle. 'Green light does that to a girl. It doesn't make you look too bad yourself—and you have sixteen stitches in your head and a day's beard growth.'

'So I have.' He grinned and put a hand to his jaw. 'So you're seeing me at my best. Out of green light, without my stitches and after-five shadow…'

'I probably won't be half so smitten.'

'You're smitten?' His voice was hopeful, and she chuckled again.

Keep it light…

'For the moment. While you're green.'

'You won't love me tomorrow?'

She closed her eyes and the laughter died. 'You and I both know there's no tomorrow in all of this, Dev Macafferty,' she said simply, but there was pain behind her words. 'This is just…just momentary. I've been on this island for too long…'

'Meaning you're sex-starved?' It was impossible to keep the note of hope from his voice, and she managed laughter again.

'In your dreams, Dev Macafferty. A kiss is one thing, but if you think I'm leaping into bed with you…'

'I can only hope.'

'Well, hope away. Besides, you have a son to be moral in front of now.'

'Maggie…'

'No!' She pulled back, a trace of panic entering her eyes as his voice grew serious. 'No, Dev, I don't want...'

'To be kissed?'

'I don't want attachments.'

'Why? Because you're already attached?' His hand came down and caught hers, pulling it up so her wedding ring gleamed in the moonlight. 'To your husband? Where is he, Maggie?'

There was only one answer to that, and it hurt. 'He's...Michael's dead.'

Silence.

'I'm sorry,' he said at last, his eyes not leaving hers. He'd known there were boogies up here—ghosts—and here was the worst ghost he could possibly imagine. He could see the memory of her husband flooding Maggie's face with pain, hauling her back from this magic night—from what lay between them.

'I...don't be. I...'

'How long ago?'

'Six months.'

Not long, then. Not long enough.

'It's me...it's me who should be sorry,' she said, shoving pain back and opening her eyes wide. She even managed a smile. 'Using you...letting you kiss me...'

'It did feel good,' he said softly. Keep it light, he told himself, just as she had. That was the way she obviously wanted it, and he had no choice but to follow.

'It did.' She stood on her tiptoes and her lips lightly brushed his. 'It does, and I'm grateful...for you making me feel like a woman again. Sometimes...sometimes I almost forget.'

'You're every inch a woman, Maggie.'

'I am,' she said regretfully. 'And sometimes I ache...' She stopped and shook her head, fighting off a bad dream.

'Well, that's no business of yours. I'm going down now. Are you coming too—or will you stay and keep the boogies company?'

'No.' He sighed and put his hand out to trace the line of her cheek. 'I'll come down. Somehow I don't think the boogies will stay up here with me. I think they'll be following you.'

CHAPTER FIVE

MAGGIE hardly slept, and she welcomed the dawn as a friend. Night meant the shadows became horror, and she couldn't get away from them. She'd forgotten them momentarily last night, in Dev's arms, but the moment she'd left him they'd flooded back, and now there was added guilt…

She was going nuts, she decided bitterly, waking herself up with a cold shower, then hauling on jeans and sweatshirt. She was turning into a guilt-ridden hermit, and wouldn't Michael just love it if he could see that? Her punishment would be complete.

She brushed her curls and hauled them back, her gaze catching her wedding ring as she did. She should haul it off, she told herself crossly, and her right hand moved to do just that—and then pulled away again.

'You still feel married,' she told her reflection. 'He's still holding on…'

Goats. Milking. A cup of tea for Grandpa before she left. Work was what she needed. Therein lay her salvation.

Work until I'm a hundred? she asked herself, as she whistled to Lucy and trudged out across the island to bring in the goats. I can just see me as an old lady, with my smelly goats and my smelly seaweed and my too expensive cheeses and my dog…

Lucy put her nose in her hand and looked worried, and Maggie grimaced.

'Yeah, you won't be here, will you, girl? In fifty years I'll be eighty, you'll be gone, Grandpa will be gone, even

Ernestine... Good grief, you'll be blubbering next,' she said out loud. 'And it's all because of *that man...*'

No. All Dev had done was wake her to the fact that she was still a woman and she still had needs.

Dev...

Whew! She needed another cold shower, she thought as she trudged on. He made her feel...

Every inch a woman?

Which is something I can't let myself feel ever again, she told herself. For heaven's sake, Maggie, stop being a dope. You've been down that road before, and look where it got you.

Dev's different.

He's a man. What's more, he's rich and powerful and way, way out of your league. Just like Michael. So think. Firstly, there's no way you ever want a man on a power kick again, and secondly...there's no way he'll want anything to do with you after this week. Last night was pure animal need...

It was really strong animal need. Admit it. So maybe...

Maybe she could hang up her inhibitions and enjoy herself for a week, she thought dubiously, thinking it through. Maybe she could accept the rest of her life after that. There was time enough for loneliness in the future...

The wedding band was still on her finger. She twisted it, but it stayed right where it was.

Time enough for loneliness in the future?

That time was now.

Dev woke to a small, insistent finger lifting one of his eyelids. He opened the other, to find Dominic three inches from his nose.

'I was just seeing if you were awake,' he said in a scared little whisper, and Dev knew the child expected a rebuff.

He got no such thing. Dev fought back a yawn, grinned a welcome and threw back the covers to invite his son in.

'Cold feet? Come and join me?'

'What…get in with you?'

'It seems sensible.'

'I never have,' Dom said gravely, looking at his father with huge eyes. 'Got into bed with a grown-up, I mean.'

'Not even with your mother?'

'Gay doesn't let me in her bedroom. But…I can't find Lucy and I don't even have my computer…' He tried to suppress a tiny sob, but it came out anyway. His computer… His only friend.

Dev's arms reached out and took Dom by the waist, hauled him up into the bed beside him and covered them both with blankets. Then they lay back on the pillows, original and miniature Macaffertys side by side, staring intently at the ceiling while Dom got himself back under control.

'You'll have to help me choose you another computer when we get to the mainland,' Dev said finally. 'And I reckon Lucy might have gone to the dairy with Maggie.'

'Why?'

'It's Lucy's job to herd the goats.'

'Oh.' Dom's face cleared. 'I expect you're right.' He frowned and his nose wrinkled. 'Dad…'

Dev wasn't used to the word. It still gave him a kick in the guts when he heard it—a strange feeling of fear and joy.

'Yep?'

'When we get to Tasmania, after we leave here, where will we live?'

'I have a house near Hobart. It's a big old house that looks out over the river, on a farm, with lots of rooms and a huge garden.'

'Room for a computer?'

'Definitely.'

'Who else lives there?'

'My two aunts. They're your two great-aunts, Myrtle and Molly. They're nutty, but nice.' How would the aunts take to Dominic? he wondered. They'd probably overwhelm him—if he could persuade them to stay. If he could, then they'd take Dominic on as a challenge.

Dear heaven… It made him tired just to think about that. The aunts' challenges were a challenge all by themselves. If they decided Dominic needed mothering, heaven help Dominic.

'What do you mean, nutty but nice?' Once more, Dominic's small nose wrinkled as he thought over Dev's words. 'Like Maggie?'

'They're a bit different.' Comparing Myrtle and Molly to Maggie… The aunts were a law unto themselves—but then so was Maggie. The three Ms.

Only Maggie wasn't an elderly spinster. The thought, for some reason, was totally abhorrent.

'I wish we could live with Maggie.' Dominic took a deep breath. 'Maggie's like a proper mother.'

Dev's heart stilled. 'Dom, you have a proper mother. Gay's your mother.'

'No. She doesn't want me,' Dom said matter-of-factly. 'She won't even let me call her Mum. She said I just get in the way of her life, and she should have let you keep me in the first place.' His strange little smile played out again, as if he had a good secret. 'She said…'

'Yes?'

'She said you wanted me ever since I was a baby, and you would have kept me if she'd let you. She said it was just to make you feel bad that she didn't let you have me, and…and something about bleeding you dry… But you really wanted me. Is that true?'

Dev lay back on the pillows and let this sink in—and then he let his breath out in a long sigh of relief. Here, then, was an unexpected gift. Gay might have been a dreadful mother, but in her malice she'd given her son something to hold to—the knowledge that his father wanted him. Dominic might have been starved of joy, but in the back of his mind he'd known that Dev loved him.

It was a gift to both of them, Dev thought silently, watching Dominic's face. It explained why Dominic was so open to him now—and how great a gift was that? Magic!

Dev's arm came out and wrapped Dom very firmly to him, and he held him tight.

'Dom, your mother's right. I've always wanted you,' he said softly. 'You're my son. Part of me. You know your mother left me before you were even born? I never met you until you were two years old, but still I wanted you. The lawyers let your mother have you, but there wasn't a day I didn't want you with me.'

'I thought so,' Dom said in satisfaction. 'You're not going to cry, are you?'

'Why should I cry?'

'I don't know, but you've got that funny, wet sound behind your voice, like Greg gets when he's drunk and Gay says she'll leave him.'

'Dom, I won't leave you.'

'I expect you will,' Dom said, and he sounded so old for his age that it was all Dev could do not to act just like the soggy Greg. And cry. 'But it's good we're stuck here, so you can't, and when we get to Hobart you'll still buy me a computer, just for me. Promise?'

'Yes. I promise.' It was all he could think of to say. 'But I won't leave you.' And then Dev thought of the next six months, and his business commitments—and how on earth was he going to manage everything? And what had he just promised, for heaven's sake?

'Yeah, right.' Dominic's tone held cynicism. Dev's promise had obviously been taken for what it was worth, and Dev wouldn't be held to it. Dom wriggled his toes and looked seriously at the ceiling. Then he wriggled his toes some more. This sleeping in was all very well, but... 'Are we going to stay in bed all day?'

'I thought we could stay a while longer.'

'Maggie's working.' It was an accusation, and Dev sighed.

'You want us to get up and help?'

'Mmm. And I'm hungry.'

It seemed there was no choice.

'Okay, twerp. We'll get up.'

'That's great, because I bet Maggie's waiting for us. She needs us to help her.'

And maybe that was true, too, Dev thought ruefully, thinking of Maggie's haunted face as he slid out from the warmth and headed for his own cold shower—but how could they help her?

There were too many problems crowding in. He stood under the cold water and waited for the mist to clear, but it didn't work. He dried himself, feeling just as confused as ever. His life at the moment was like some crazy jigsaw puzzle that had been tipped upside down and had the pieces altered.

How on earth was he going to get it back together again—and what would it look like when he did?

Joe was in the kitchen when they emerged, calmly making toast on the fire. Dominic looked at the toasting fork and sighed—but then hiked over to the table and started chopping himself a slab of bread. Dev had to grin. Kids were nothing if not adaptable.

'Sleep all right?' Joe demanded, and Dev nodded.

'Very well, sir.'

'Joe, not sir,' Joe snapped. 'Your leg made it all the way up the lighthouse and back, then?'

He knew. 'Yes.'

'Did you kiss her?' Joe went on calmly.

'I beg your pardon?'

'You heard,' Joe said calmly.

'I… Joe, I can't…' Dev shook his head and Joe's eyes narrowed.

'Maggie won't tell me either,' he said dourly. 'I asked her when she brought me in a cup of tea and she blushed beetroot. Now you've gone quiet. Guess that means you did.'

'Joe…'

'The girl needs kissing,' Joe went on, satisfied. 'Damned island…it's no place for a girl her age.'

'Maybe it's a good place for her to get over her husband's death,' Dev said softly, moving to take the bread knife from his son and chop some slices that didn't resemble bricks.

'Ha! Michael!'

'You didn't like him?' He had no business to ask, but he was asking all the same.

'Wimp,' Joe said contemptuously and bent to toss another log into the stove. 'Okay, boy.' He handed the toasting fork to Dominic. 'Your turn. I charred mine. See if you can do better.'

'I can't see Maggie married to a wimp,' Dev said cautiously, and was rewarded with another snort.

'Yeah, well, maybe he wasn't—when Maggie married him. Or maybe he was and she just couldn't see. She was young, a long way from home and too damned innocent for words. Her grandma and me brought her up here on the island after her parents died, and from the time she was ten she hardly saw another person. She did her schooling by correspondence and then she took off to Melbourne to do her nursing, but she was like a fish out of water in the big city. Hannah…that's my wife…was *that* worried about her, but then she met Michael…'

He paused to jab jam onto his toast, and the way he jabbed it, it looked as if he'd like to jab something else. Or someone else.

'And they married?'

'And they married.' Joe sighed. 'Well, I could see why she fell for him, and Hannah reckoned it'd be okay. He was a hot-shot surgeon, good-looking, rich, gift of the gab—and it was only me who worried why he'd take up with a kid barely out of the schoolroom. But he looked after her, and made her happy for a while. It was only after…'

He paused, and then he sighed again. 'Well, Maggie grew up, didn't she? And Michael didn't like it. He wanted her to stay just the same—a scared kid, totally reliant on him. But Maggie had only been scared for the first bit…she's not a scared woman.'

'I can see that,' Dev said dryly.

'So they fought,' Joe said. 'There were some rip-snorters of fights, though she never told us about them—but Hannah reckoned she could tell…by her letters, I mean. Not by what she said, but by what she didn't say.'

'And then he died?'

'It wasn't as simple as that,' Joe said grimly. 'She left him, you see. I don't know why. Hannah was dead, I'd had the stroke and was in some hospital on the mainland, and next thing Maggie was taking over the dairy here until I was well enough to come home. Then she was picking up my gear and saying, "Come on, we're going back to the island, both of us." I said, "What about Michael? and she said Michael wasn't part of her life any more. I wasn't given any say in the matter. I was just brought home.'

'You didn't want to come?' Dev frowned.

'I won't say that,' Joe said grimly. 'Though it's been damned lonely here since Hannah died. I didn't want to go into some nursing home, but I'd sort of thought... Maggie and Michael had a big house, with heaps of extra rooms, and I thought maybe we could sell the lease here to someone who wanted to keep on with the cheese, and me and Lucy...' He sighed again. 'But of course if they were fighting it wouldn't have worked. But then we got back here and Michael went and killed himself.'

'Killed himself!'

'He never meant to,' Joe said quickly, seeing Dev's horrified look. 'At last, I don't think he did, but Maggie won't say. He had some fancy car—a Ferrari sports job that'd go like a bushfire—and he got himself drunk and hit a tree. It happened three days after we got back here—and know what? Maggie wouldn't even leave me to go to the funeral. She just sort of went quiet—silent. She's been like a ghost ever since, trying not to let me see it, but she hurts. And he's supposed to have had all this money but there's not a sign of it. Not a penny. We're as poor as church mice, which never worried me and Hannah, but it worries me when it means Maggie's stuck here with not even the means to give the place a coat of paint.'

He shrugged. 'So there you are, boy. You now know as much as me, which isn't very much at all. Maggie tells me nothing. What are you going to do with it?'

'I guess the same as you...nothing,' Dev said, watching Dominic adjust his bread on the fork and hold it to the flames. 'It's Maggie's business.'

'You kissed her last night.'

'Yes, but…'

'She's a fine woman.' Joe poked a finger towards Dominic. 'The boy needs a mother.'

'Joe!'

'It's true,' Joe said dourly. 'Anyone can see that.'

'I have two aunts who'll give him all the mothering he'll need.'

'Yeah? How old are they?'

'Molly's sixty-nine and Myrtle's seventy.' Dev frowned as he thought of Molly and Myrtle and mothering. They were great at what they did, but…mothering? More like smothering.

'Then they'll be grandmothers,' Joe said flatly, discarding the unknown Molly and Myrtle with four words. 'Got anyone else lined up?'

'No, but…'

'Then what are you waiting for,' Joe said savagely. He swiped his jam knife across his toast to apply an extra layer. 'Get on with it. That's the trouble with the younger generation. You don't see a gift horse when it's staring you in the face. And my Maggie's a gift horse. You could search the world and not find a better lass.'

'Dad?'

'Mmm?' Breakfasted, Dev and Dom walked across the island to the dairy, with Dominic manfully matching Dev stride for stride. Dev was still limping, but his strides were at least twice the length of Dominic's.

He'd shortened his steps when he realised what his son was doing, but he'd been firmly told to lengthen them again. 'I can do it,' Dom had said, and marched on. Now he was deep in thought, but still at full stretch.

'What does Grandpa mean when he says Maggie's a gift horse?' he demanded.

'Grandpa? His name's Mr Cray.'

'He told me to call him Grandpa,' Dom said stubbornly. 'He says he likes it. Tell me why Maggie's a gift horse.'

'He means he likes her.'

'No.' Dom thought this through and rejected it. 'He means he's giving her to you.'

'You know as well as me that you can't give people away.'

'Gay and Greg gave me away.'

'They didn't.'

'Yes, they did. They took me to that boarding school because they didn't want me, and then when the school said I couldn't stay they gave me to you.'

'Dom...'

'So you can give people away, and Grandpa's giving Maggie to us.'

'I think you might find,' Dev said carefully, 'that Maggie would be hurt if she heard you say that. She loves her grandpa and he loves her.'

'Yeah.' Dom thought that through and found it reasonable. 'I didn't like it when I figured out that Gay didn't like me. But this'd be different. We could love Maggie.'

'No...'

'Yes, we could,' Dom said triumphantly. 'Because Grandpa said you kissed her, and every time Gay kisses someone she says she loves them.'

'I'm a bit different from your mother.' Dev's voice was suddenly clipped, and any colleague would have known to back off right now. Dominic, however, knew no such restraint.

'If you kissed her then you could marry her,' he said persuasively.

'I'm not a marrying man.'

'Yes, you are. You married Gay.'

And that's why I'm no longer a marrying man, Dev thought silently, but out loud he somehow forced his voice to stay light.

'Dominic, there's no way we could take Maggie away from here,' he said. 'She has thirty goats, and she has Lucy and she has her grandpa.'

'She'd like us better.'

'They need her, Dom,' Dev said gently. 'It's not fair of us to even think about taking her away.'

But suddenly…he was thinking about it. An idea was forming in the back of his mind as if a brilliant lightbulb had suddenly turned on. It was absolutely crazy, and he knew it was crazy, but it was there for all that. Maybe…

No. Ridiculous!

It wouldn't go away.

Molly and Myrtle and Ernestine Goat, and Joe and Lucy and Maggie and Dominic—all neatly packaged in one glorious solution.

It was so crazy that it might just work!

Maggie was ushering in her last six goats to the milking stalls when they arrived at the dairy, and she greeted them with wary delight. Or maybe she greeted Dominic with the delight part, and Dev with the wary bit.

'Do you want to help put the cups on their teats?' she asked Dom, as he scuttled across to her side. He nodded, his small body settling in close, and he gave his father a look that was almost defiant.

See, his look said. She's ours. She belongs to us…

'Aren't they touchy?' Dev asked, unsuccessfully trying to push away the crazy thoughts his son had started. 'Any cow I've ever milked has taken weeks to get used to a stranger in the dairy.'

'You're not touchy, are you, girls?' Maggie patted the rump of one of the goats as she nosed into the feed trough and presented her udder for milking. 'Not unless you scare them, and then they tend to overreact.'

'Like how?'

'Like they drop dead.'

'You're kidding!'

'Nope. They're odd animals. They're tough as old boots unless they're stressed, and then their answer is to lie down and die.' Maggie chuckled. 'They wouldn't fit into the cut and thrust of your modern business world, Mr Macafferty.'

'I suppose not,' he said blankly.

'I'd never try to take them off the island, either,' she said. 'It'd stress them so much I might lose a quarter of them in the process.'

So Molly and Myrtle would just have to come here. Molly and Myrtle and Windswept Cheeses... Dev's mind was still in overdrive. That might fit. They might just love it.

'Why are you looking like that?' Maggie said suddenly, her eyes narrowing.

'Like what?'

'Like you're adding up balance sheets in your head.'

'I'm not...'

'If you want to be useful, go and wash peppercorns.'

'I beg your pardon?'

'There's a pile of dried peppercorns in the processing room,' she said. 'Each one has to be carefully washed to make sure there are no impurities and there's no residual dust.'

'Why?'

'After I finish milking I'm packing cheese,' she said pa-

tiently. 'I put garlic, thyme and peppercorns into each jar.'
She sighed. 'The peppercorns look lovely, and the custom-
ers expect them, but I don't think they add much flavour
and they're a pain to wash. However, what the customer
wants the customer gets…'

She brightened and cast him a challenging look. 'And
you ate our food for breakfast. Dominic is paying for his
breakfast by helping me milk, and then he can help me
sluice the dairy. Meanwhile…you can wash peppercorns
for your keep. I knew I hauled you out of that aeroplane
for a reason.'

And she gave him her very brightest smile, turned her
back on him and turned her attention back to her goats.

So Dev spent an hour carefully sorting and cleaning peppercorns, a job he'd never thought of doing in his life. He'd
never thought such a job existed. Outside, Maggie and
Dominic chatted like long-lost friends, and the idea in
Dev's head grew stronger by the minute. It had been a
mistake to leave him alone. His lightbulb turned bigger and
brighter every moment.

The milkers finished and came into the processing room,
but still Dev's mind kept working. Maggie sliced the blocks
of pressed curd and packed them into jars, and Dev and
Dom carefully, artistically, inserted thyme and garlic and
peppercorns. By mid-morning they had a hundred jars of
beautifully packed Windswept Cheese.

'Gorgeous,' Maggie said, putting her hands on her hips
and surveying her produce with satisfaction. 'That's my
work done in half the time, thanks to you guys. What do
you want to do now?'

Organise, Dev thought suddenly. Throw some proposi-
tions about. Get things moving.

It was too soon. There was still a wariness in Maggie's

eyes, he decided, and one of the reasons he was a good businessman was that he knew timing was essential. He shouldn't have kissed her last night, he thought—not if he was about to proposition her. The only thing that could get in the way of his glorious scheme was sex...

'How about a guided tour of your island?' he asked.

'What...all the way around?'

'Yes.'

'Is your leg up to it?'

'The only time my leg hurts is when I stop still,' he told her. 'It's stiff now, after sitting so long. It needs exercise.'

'Can we go all the way around the island?' Dom demanded, and Maggie smiled—her eyes still vaguely puzzled. She kept looking at Dev as if she suspected a trap.

This second sight was getting a bit wearing, Dev thought, trying to keep his face innocent. How could he organise timing if she could second guess him?

'You can,' she told him, still watching Dev. 'How about you taking your dad around? I'll see to Grandpa.'

'How about if we all see to Grandpa and then you take us for a guided tour?' Dev suggested.

That brought a grin. 'You need a guide saying this is a rock and this is a bigger rock and this...this is a really, really big rock?'

'It'd be good,' Dev said solidly. 'If I try to take Dom myself we'll end up getting lost.'

Maggie choked. 'On an island two miles long by a mile wide?'

'I get disoriented in the bath,' he told her, his lazy smile challenging. 'Come on, Maggie. All this hard work's making me feel guilty, and the only way I can stop feeling guilty is to stop you working. You want to explore the island, don't you Dom?'

'I already did,' Dom told him. 'Yesterday. I guess I can

show you the way, though.' Then he relented and looked sideways at Maggie. 'But it'd be good if you came too, Maggie. After all, it's your island.'

'Big of you.'

'It'd be better if you came,' said Dominic, and he looked at her and smiled a shy little smile—and Maggie was lost.

All right, then, she'd go, but it was just because of Dominic, she told herself helplessly. It had nothing to do with the way Dev was looking at her, too. With his lazy, twinkling smile that was totally magnetic...

She spread helpless hands. 'Heck, I'm being bulldozed by two males here. What chance does a woman have?'

'None at all,' Dev told her gravely. He reached for her hands and pulled her towards him, and somehow Dominic was caught between them. Man, woman and child... He ignored Maggie's sharp intake of breath and kept smiling right down at her. 'Let's see to Joe's needs, and then have some lunch. We'll need all our strength for exploration. After all, if we were to get lost you might be stuck with us for ever, Maggie—and that would never do. Now would it?'

'Yes, it would,' Dom said fiercely, but Maggie was shaking her head.

'You needn't worry,' she told him, and there was a trace of seriousness behind the laughter in her voice. 'You won't be stuck on the island for ever, if that's what you're worrying about. There's no way you can escape from Ernestine and the girls. They'll track you down wherever you are, and when the supply boat comes in then that'll be the end of you. You'll be carried from this island at goat-point.'

'But today,' Dominic said urgently, looking up from Dev to Maggie and back again, 'today we can have fun. Together. Right?'

'Yes,' said Maggie, and her voice was close to breathless. 'Yes, we can, Dominic Macafferty. In fact, for a week we can have fun. But after a week…you're on you own.'

And so am I, she thought grimly, and there was a cold, leaden feeling in her heart at the thought of the future. So am I…

CHAPTER SIX

It was one of the island's perfect days. The sun glimmered through high white clouds, causing the grey rocks to shine. The goats, following at sticky-nose distance, looked gorgeous themselves, the Saanens a shimmering white and the Alpines' pretty grey and white coats blending into the rocks like camouflage. The sea was almost millpond flat, the high winds of two days ago nothing more than a memory.

Maggie and Dominic led Dev around the goat track, the only path that went all around the island. They made slow progress. It wasn't Dev's limp that held them up—it was Maggie's habit of swooping into each bay to check the seaweed, or hauling up rocks to show Dom crabs, or simply showing how fast she could clamber up a bluff or two. Dominic and Lucy bounced around her, with Dominic mesmerised by her enthusiasm. Dev was simply left to watch,

'You make me feel decrepit,' he complained as Maggie and Dom bounded back from another exploration down to the sea. Dom was holding a handful of shells and a massive crab claw of some long-departed crustacean. Dom looked glowing. He'd been out of boarding school—out of his mother's control—for two days, and already he was almost deliriously happy. This island stay had almost been worth the plane crash, Dev thought.

'Decrepit?' Maggie stopped before him and eyed him from head to toe. She was wearing her faded jeans and a stained T-shirt, toes bare and her hair was hauled back again. She looked pretty and young and...free. 'Does your leg hurt?'

'No…'

'Then why do you feel decrepit?' Once more he was subjected to scrutiny. 'How old are you?'

He grinned. 'There's no need to sound so apprehensive.'

'Apprehensive?'

'As if I might say eighty. You have the tone of one addressing the very old.'

'Well?' she said innocently, skipping to a rock above the path and looking down.

'I'm thirty-four,' he said, goaded.

She gasped. 'Wow!'

'Don't tell me. You can't imagine how it must be to be that old.'

'We can't, can we, Dominic?' She held out a hand and Dom scrambled up to join her. The child's hand slid trustingly into hers, and Maggie stood gazing down at Dev and felt…alive…good…better than she'd felt for…

For a lifetime. Since Michael.

Since way, way before Michael, she thought suddenly, when she'd been a teenager and her life had been her own.

Dev sank down onto a rock and groaned. 'You know, this place would do a whole heap better with a comfy chair or two,' he told them.

'For old fogeys like you,' she agreed kindly. 'But I see what you mean. The aged need comfy chairs. Parking lots. Condominiums.' She brightened. 'I wouldn't worry. Some developer's probably got it on his list right this minute. I only hope he likes goats.'

'He'd better.' Dev shoved away Ernestine's nose from his neck and groaned. 'We'll all come back in forty years and find the place fitted with high-rise goat sheds.'

'Who's coming back? I'll still be here in forty years,' Maggie said, and her laughter slipped a little bit. Then she bit her lip, catching herself, and fought again for lightness.

'And maybe Dom will come back to visit me, but you…? No way. Forty years! Remember, you're *thirty-four* already!'

'Wretch!' Dev lifted a lump of damp seaweed from beside the path and aimed it at the laughing girl above him. It landed neatly on her head and slid down around her shoulders.

'Ugh.' Maggie wrenched the slimy stuff away. She flung it at her feet, and Lucy nosed it curiously. 'Bite him, Lucy.'

Lucy looked enquiringly up, and then put her nose down again. Dev grinned at her disobedience. 'What a thing to suggest. Lucy has principles, even if her owner doesn't.'

'You mean, Lucy has sense,' Maggie corrected him. 'I guess if I was Lucy I wouldn't bite you either. At your age you'd be as tough as old boots.' She turned her back on him, jumped down from her rock and held out her hand for Dominic to follow. 'Come on, Dom, let's keep going.' Then she turned back, as if on an afterthought.

'Are you okay to come?' she asked kindly. 'Or would you like us to go back for your bath chair? Maybe you could fetch it, Dom…and a nice shawl for your daddy's knees.'

Dev groaned as Dominic giggled. 'The younger generation are getting worse all the time,' he said. 'Don't listen to her, Dom. You need to learn a nice, healthy respect for your father.'

'Your ageing father,' Maggie added.

The ageing father shoved himself to his feet and glowered. 'Get on, wench,' he ordered. 'Move. You need to get this ageing decrepit around the island and back in time for his tea. Gruel and junket—something I can't lose my false teeth in…'

Maggie grinned, and then she hesitated. 'Dev, we really can stop if your leg is hurting,' she told him seriously.

'Maggie…' Dev's voice matched hers for seriousness.

'After the conversation we've just had, I don't intend to stop until I've been around the island three times, driving you before me.'

Maggie chuckled and led the way on. The sun was warm on her face, Dominic's hand was warm in hers, Lucy was at her heels... And Dev was right beside them.

Dev. Devlin Macafferty.

He was only here for a week, she told herself. This lightness couldn't last.

It wasn't just lightness, she thought, wondering. It was different somehow...a feeling she'd never experienced in her life before.

It had to do with the feel of Dominic's hand...with the child's chuckle, with the way his curls just kicked up at the nape of his neck...

The way his father's curls did the same.

And the way his father's mouth had felt on hers. The way her body had moulded to his. As if...dear Lord...as if it was her home.

She was going mad, she told herself blankly. Stark, staring mad. Any minute now she'd start grinning like a Cheshire cat because these two were making her feel happier than she could remember feeling in her life before.

They were only here for a week.

Plus...there was no way she wanted emotional entanglement in her life again, even if there was the remotest possibility of them staying, she told herself bleakly. No way. Ever, ever again.

Ha!

It took two more days before Dev's wonderful idea surfaced—two days where he and Dominic worked beside her, milking, cheese making, scrubbing jars, sluicing the dairy, tending goats, hauling bull kelp off the beach to dry on the racks above the high water line, helping Joe learn to walk again…

All the time Dev was thinking over and over his plan, and everything he learned about her in those two days made him think it could work. Maggie was one special woman. He could offer her a life.

And the sex thing?

Well, maybe that could work as well—or not work, which was more appropriate. After that one stupid time up in the lighthouse, she'd held herself aloof from him, and he knew she wanted emotional entanglements as little as he did. Or as little as he had…

No. It had to be a business proposition, he thought firmly. That was what it must be if it had any chance of working at all.

Tuesday night.

Joe and Dominic were safely in bed, Lucy was asleep before the fire in the tiny living room, Maggie was curled up beside her with a book, seemingly oblivious to Dev's presence—and Dev was just watching. Waiting. Watching the firelight flicker over her face, the fine lines of her cheeks shadowed by the mass of curls tumbling free.

He wanted to touch her, he thought suddenly—fiercely—and it took a Herculean effort to stay on the other side of the room.

Business! This was business, he told himself. Nothing else.

'Maggie?'

She looked up and smiled at him, and once more the urge hit home. She was so lovely…

Business!

'I was wondering…'

'Yes?'

Why was it so hard to say it? Because it was important, he thought—desperately important. The future of six people hinged on her response.

'I've been thinking…'

'Amazing!' Her eyes danced and he drew in his breath. Her loveliness wasn't making it any easier to be business-like.

'There's no need to be cynical.'

'No.' She schooled her face into one of polite interest. 'No, of course not, Mr Macafferty. You've been thinking. I'm impressed. Tell me what you've thought.'

'I…' Damn. If she was going to laugh… 'Maggie?'

'Yes?' She was being schoolmarm to his slightly dim-witted student. Good grief, she was patronising him here.

He wanted to smile—but he didn't. He couldn't. This was too important for laughter, and the longer he waited the more important it seemed. He stood and crossed to the fire, but he didn't look down at her—just stood with his back to the fire and stared out through the darkened window, as if he could see into the night beyond.

Putting laughter away in the search his future…

'Maggie, I was wondering if you'd marry me.'

Silence.

The silence stretched on and on, endless in its confusion. The word echoed around them into the night. Marry…

Finally Maggie moistened suddenly dry lips and laid her book aside. She was reading a book labelled *Goat Husbandry*. Frivolous stuff…

'I have to assume you're joking,' she said softly, in a voice that sounded as if all the breath had been sucked from it.

'I'm not joking.'

'Then you're nuts.' She didn't rise, just stayed seated at his feet, her wonderful skirt splayed on the floor around her. She looked up at him—Jane Eyre in person—and it was all Dev could do not to reach down and gather her up to him.

She'd disappear if he did. He knew enough of this woman to know that emotion was the last thing she wanted. She was fey—a spirit thing—and the only way to capture her was by keeping his own feet firmly on the ground.

'I'm not nuts, Maggie,' he said evenly. 'I've thought this through over the last few days, and the more I think about it the more sensible it seems.'

'Yeah?'

'Yeah.'

She closed her eyes, and then slowly rose to her feet, backing away from him as if he was growing antennae before her eyes. 'Dev, this is crazy. You don't even know me.'

'I know enough of you to know you're the wife I want, Maggie,' he said evenly, schooling himself to stay still. 'You're warm, compassionate, funny, caring…you have a heart as big as any woman's I've ever met.'

'You don't…you're not saying you've fallen in love with me?'

'No.' Had he? Dev didn't want to look too closely at that one. Therein lay all the complications he didn't want. 'Maggie, I know you've been through the mill…'

'I have,' she said savagely, anger flooding her face. 'Dev, this is ridiculous. I've been a possession for ten long years, and there's no way I'm buying into that again.'

'A possession…' He frowned. 'Explain that to me, Maggie. I don't understand.'

'It's easy enough. Michael thought he owned me,' she said flatly. 'Oh, I should have known when he married me, but I was stupid. He was so proud of me, just like a piece of Dresden china. I was a possession. He told me what to wear, he told me how to behave… Everything! Even going to the polling booth on election day was torture to Michael because he wasn't allowed to fill in my voting slip for me— and if I tried to make my own friends…or look sideways at another man… And all the time…all the time if I tried to break the bonds he'd fall into a heap. ''I'll die without you, Maggie,'' he told me, and finally he did.'

'Hey, Maggie, I'm not asking…'

'It was only Grandpa who set me free,' she went on, as if she hadn't heard his interruption. 'It was when Grandpa needed me so desperately—but Michael couldn't bear to share. He hated me working. He wouldn't let us have children because that'd be sharing, and then he wouldn't have me bring Grandpa home when he was so ill. So in the end… Michael was saying he'd die without me, but I saw Grandpa in hospital and I knew that in a nursing home, without people who loved him, Grandpa really would die. So I chose. And Michael carried out his threat. So now Michael's making me pay, and as for marriage again…'

'Maggie…'

'He was rich, you know,' Maggie continued. 'Filthy rich—but there's no way I'd ever touch his money. I've sent it all to a cancer care unit. I walked away from him with nothing. I just couldn't…'

And her voice broke on a sob.

It was too much. Dev had steeled himself not to touch her, but a man would have to be inhuman not to move now—not to take her into his arms and hold her against him and stroke that lovely hair…

'Maggie, don't cry… Hey, you can't cry. He must have been sick. Crazy…'

'He was sick,' she said brokenly. 'I knew that. I tried to make him see, but he wouldn't. He was so powerful.' She hauled herself out of Dev's hold and looked up at him, willing him to understand. 'He was so powerful, so good-looking, tall, with a shock of silver hair... Everyone thought he was wonderful...they told me how lucky I was to be married to someone so strong... And then I'd say I was leaving him and he'd cry...'

'It was blackmail,' Dev said disgustedly, and Maggie nodded.

'Yes, but it worked. For ten long years it worked.' She took a ragged breath, tilted her chin and stared at him with defiance. 'I knew he meant it, you see, and he did. So...there's no way I want marriage again, Dev. If there's any emotional entanglement, then I'm out of here. I'm free. Apart from Michael's ghost...'

'You don't mean you still feel guilty?'

'He killed himself,' she said dully. 'The police say he ran off the road—but he killed himself. Because of me.'

'Then that's still blackmail,' he said strongly, gripping her shoulders and willing her to keep her eyes on his. 'Maggie, he was trying to punish you in the worst way he knew. He didn't die because of you. He died because of him. It was his decision to end his life—not yours. You can't feel guilty.'

'Dev, don't...' She pulled back and her hands fell uselessly to her sides, as if she didn't know where to put them. 'I don't know why I told you. I haven't told anyone else. Not even Grandpa.'

'You should have.'

'I didn't.' Once more her chin came up. 'But marriage to you...it's crazy. I don't know what sort of stupid plan you have in your head...'

'It's a practical plan.'

'But...'

'It's not emotional at all,' he told her quickly—though that wasn't the way he was feeling. He was feeling so emotional here he was close to tearing in two himself. 'Maggie, sit down.'

'I don't want…'

Once more he gripped her shoulders, but this time it was to propel her onto the settee. He knelt then, and took her hands in his, his broad, strong hands feeding her warmth. 'No. Don't tell me what you don't want. Just listen. First to what I don't want either. I don't want emotional entanglements, Maggie. I don't want a wife in the real sense of the word. But I desperately need a mother for Dominic.'

'He has a mother,' she said flatly.

'No.'

'But…'

'Gay didn't want him.' Dev sighed, and his fingers moved in hers. 'Gay and I had an affair. We were young, just out for a good time, and it had barely started before it ended. But Gay found herself pregnant.' He shrugged. 'I had a farm up north and Gay was the daughter of my next-door neighbour. She was desperate to get away from the little farming community where she'd grown up. Unfortunately her mother was widowed, rich and domineering. She wouldn't give Gay a cent and Gay felt trapped. Maybe…it was because I felt sorry for her that we started the affair.'

'And then?' Maggie said, caught despite herself. The aching misery in her eyes had been replaced by sympathy.

'Well, because we'd taken precautions and thought we were safe, Gay was over four months pregnant before she realised. When she did she was horrified. It seemed the only course for us was to marry, so we did, but then two weeks after we married her mother died. Gay inherited her mother's farm and fortune, and she turned on me like I'd planned everything. I'd trapped her into marriage before she'd inherited, she said—so she walked away.'

Dev sighed again. 'Maggie, I was young and irrespon-

sible and after Gay left I was a carefree bachelor again—
but when Dom was born I achingly wanted my son. So
much so that it took over my life. I was stupid, though. I
told Gay I wanted him and Gay was still angry—so she
punished me the only way she knew how. She employed
expensive lawyers and she fought me at every turn for custody, but not because she wanted Dominic. It was a way
of getting back at her background—at me, and through me
at her dead parents.'

'But surely…'

'Surely nothing,' Dev said roughly. 'Dom's had expensive schools, expensive nannies, expensive houses to live
in—mostly paid for by me—but I've only seen him four
times in his life, and each time I've had to fight her tooth
and nail to get that. Each time I saw her with him I knew
she didn't want him, and he knows that. Thank God, he
knows I want him, but he needs more. He needs a proper
mother, Maggie—a mum who'll hold his hand and make
him laugh and be there…'

'You can employ a nanny.'

'No. He's had nannies. He needs you.'

Maggie took a deep breath. She eyed him dubiously, as
if the antennae might still be readying to sprout. As if he'd
zoomed in from Mars and she didn't know what the heck
to make of him. 'Dominic says you have aunts living with
you.'

He grinned then, seriousness fading. 'Yep. Molly and
Myrtle. And that's the next part of my plan.'

'I see. Or rather, I don't see.' She pulled her hands from
his, but she stayed listening, obviously decided to humour
him. Wasn't that what you were supposed to do with lu-
natics?

'That's right, you don't see.' Dev's grin deepened. 'How
could you? Maggie, I'm not just asking you to marry me.'

'You mean you're asking someone else as well?'

'There are six people in my plan,' he said softly. He rose and sat beside her on the settee. 'I haven't forgotten Joe, either.'

'Joe?'

'You can't leave him here.'

'He wants to be here.'

'No, he doesn't,' Dev told her. 'Or not specially. Joe wants company and comfort. That's more important to him than his island. He wants Lucy and he wants a fireside; he wants people to talk to and he wants warmth and care. If you'll marry me then he could come to Hobart with us. I'm no Michael. Dominic and I can share.'

'But…'

'But your goats,' Dev said in satisfaction. 'That's the next bit. The best bit. Joe worries about his goats, and I'd hate to see them leave the island—and I have the solution. The aunts.'

'The aunts…'

'My aunts are wonderful,' Dev told her. 'They've been two of the most powerful businesswomen in the land. One's been managing director of a supermarket chain; the other's been operating a massive cattle station up in Queensland. She inherited it from my grandfather with three hundred head of cattle—by the time she retired she was running thirty thousand. Anyway, three months ago they decided to retire together, return to Tasmania and look after me in their old age.'

'And what's wrong with that?'

'What's wrong is that they're driving me crazy,' Dev said frankly. 'They're putting their combined energy into running my house, my garden, my love life and my business concerns—and I can't stand it. They're like two mini-tornadoes. I get the Spanish Inquisition on each and every one of my business deals the minute I get in the door—and then I get so much advice I can't handle it. And the cooking!'

'What's wrong with cooking?'

'Nothing. In moderation. But the aunts don't know the word "moderation". Imagine cooking and cleaning and gardening and organising all multiplied by two tornadoes. My sheets are changed twice a day, my bedside drawers have been reorganised three times—Maggie, if they don't find somewhere to channel their energy soon, I'll brain them. Or they'll brain each other. They are feisty, independent women, and I had one look at your cheese making enterprise and it screamed Molly and Myrtle. They would love it!'

'You couldn't put two elderly women on this island.'

'This island is made for these two elderly women. On the mainland I'm expecting revolution any minute. Here they could reign supreme!'

'They sound wonderful.'

'They are wonderful, but they need a challenge and this could be it.'

'But...'

'And then it'd still be here for us,' Dev told her triumphantly, producing his trump card. 'We could visit whenever we wanted. I'd buy a helicopter so we could visit at will, and bring the aunts support if and when they need it. We could bring Joe here whenever he wants and give the aunts holidays—if they want them, which I'll bet they won't—while we stay here with Dom and let him run free. It's a child's paradise, Maggie. With you and me...with Joe and the aunts...we'd be a family.'

This was starting to sound real! Maggie stared at him and felt like pinching herself to make sure she was awake. His eyes twinkled back—daring her to take the challenge.

'You're never serious.'

'I'm deadly serious, Maggie.' And his voice told her he spoke the truth.

'In most families,' she said carefully, and the strain was showing in her voice, 'the mother and father have some sort of relationship.'

'We have a relationship.'

'You mean we've kissed—once.'

'Do you want more than that?' he asked, and watched her face. He had his answer. There was the instant panic.

'No. No way. I told you…'

'Then there's no problem. I'm sorry I kissed you, Maggie. I shouldn't have.'

He shouldn't have. Maggie stared blankly at him and tried to make sense of the words. She couldn't.

He saw it. He knew her well enough now to know she was all at sea, and talk would do no more than confuse her. Instead he rose, took her hands again and drew her up to stand numbly before him.

'That's it, Maggie. I'll not put any more pressure on you tonight. But…think about it, will you? Think about how good it could be, and how it could solve all our problems. Sleep on it and let me know. I'm a patient man, Maggie. I can wait.'

'Like…how long?'

'For as long as it takes,' he said gently. 'I want you as my wife, Maggie, and I have all the time in the world.'

'Oh, yeah,' she said breathlessly. 'You mean you have all the time in the world as long as I decide by the time the supply boat comes in.'

That's right.' He grinned. 'That's three days. Three days to consider the chance of a lifetime. It's heaps of time.'

'Dev…'

'Don't say a word,' he told her firmly, taking her shoulders and pushing her out through the door. 'Go to bed and sleep on it. That's all I ask.'

CHAPTER SEVEN

IT WAS an impossible task. Oh, the first part she did just fine. Go to bed... That was easy. Especially as the alternative was to sit up with Dev.

It was the second part that was impossible. Sleep... Maggie lay in the bed she'd slept in as a child; she stared at the ceiling, she hugged Lucy, who'd followed her to bed, and she'd never felt less like sleep in her life.

Marriage...

'It scares me stupid, Lucy,' she whispered to the sleepy dog. 'My marriage was a prison for ten long years. There's no way I'm going back to that.'

Dev's different. It wasn't Lucy answering. It was her own heart.

'This isn't Dev we're talking about,' she said desperately into the night. 'This is *marriage.*'

But...it wouldn't be a marriage like marriage to Michael. Dev wouldn't try to control you.

'How do you know?'

I know.

'Oh, yeah? You're so smart. You're the same woman who married Michael—remember?'

The thought made her shiver. She hugged the dog closer. Lucy roused herself to give her a sleepy lick and then left her to her deliberations while she caught up on zs. Whatever decision Maggie made, she'd be making it on her own.

Okay. What were the factors here? Comparing Michael to Dev...

Michael didn't love you.

'Neither does Dev,' she told the sleeping dog. 'This is a marriage of convenience we're talking of—nothing more. He's organising a future for his son. Off-loading responsibility for his aunts. Shirking...'

'No. He's doing sensible things for a sensible future.

'He should look after Dominic himself...'

But then the thought of Dominic's little face drifted into her heart and stayed. What Dev had said was true. The child needed both mother and father. He needed all the love he could get, and he was the child Maggie had always longed for. Even in these few days he'd blossomed, and in a stable, loving home...

'It wouldn't be stable,' she told herself crossly. 'Dev will be off around the world on his business trips, while...'

While Dom stayed with her. Not with a nanny, who was paid to care, but with Maggie, who longed for children herself and who wanted so much to be able to care...

As if on cue, there was a muffled, watery sob from the room next door. Dominic... She hadn't heard Dev come to bed, so he must still be in the sitting room at the other end of the house. He wouldn't hear—so she pushed off her bedcovers, apologised as Lucy wuffled her annoyance, and padded through next door in her long nightgown and bare feet.

Dominic was as far under the bedclothes as he could go—a solid little hump at the foot of the bed. The hump was exuding misery.

'Hey, Dom...'

Nothing.

Maggie sat on the bed and patted the hump. The hump heaved and sniffed again.

'Dom?'

'I'm sorry.'

It was a plaintive little sentence and it made Maggie's heart turn over.

'What on earth are you sorry for, rabbit?'

'Because I woke you up.'

'You didn't wake me, and even if you did… Dom, there's no need to be sorry if you're crying.'

'If I cry and wake Gay she gets angry, and if I cry at school the kids tease me.'

More heart twisting, and Maggie could bear it no longer. She pulled back the covers and hauled the sodden little urchin into her arms, nestling his curls under her chin.

'Hey, Dom, there's no way I'll get angry if you cry. If you're unhappy it's okay to let it out. You're eight years old. It's fine to howl every now and then. I'm twenty-nine and I still do.'

He huddled into her. 'Really?'

'Really. When I'm unhappy I hug Lucy and howl until she drips tears.'

'Why do you get unhappy?'

'For all sorts of things,' Maggie said softly. 'I guess…mostly because I'm lonely. Is that why you're crying, Dom? Are you lonely?'

'Lucy's not here.'

'She's asleep on my bed. Shall I whistle her for you?'

'No.' Dom sighed and nestled closer. 'You're just as good.'

'Gee, thanks.'

'I don't want to go away from here.'

Maggie closed her eyes and hugged, and then she hugged harder. This was just plain impossible!

No, it wasn't. Her eyes flew wide again and she stared over Dominic's head though the window to the moonlit sea beyond. Maybe Dev's suggestion wasn't as crazy as she'd thought.

Maybe the only thing stopping her taking a sensible course of action here was her own stupid heart.

There was a chance Dev was right and marriage didn't have to be an emotional thing, she thought. Maybe it could be a business proposition. Separate lives—but everything else fitting into place. Maybe she should give Dev's plan a hearing.

Maybe…

She hugged Dominic and crooned silly little songs while he drifted off to sleep in her arms—and she thought and thought.

Okay. Let's consider problems one at a time, she told herself.

First, Dev's right when he says Grandpa's never going to be fit and healthy again, and maybe Grandpa could be happy on the mainland. If he had me, and he had Lucy and Dominic to keep him interested… Maybe he'd be less lonely than he is now, when I need to spend so much time with the goats.

Tick Grandpa.

Dominic? That was easy.

I can love Dominic like my own. Cuddling him now… I feel like a mother hen with my chick. She hugged him close. It was almost crazy the way she was feeling about him. She loved Dom and Dom needed her.

Tick Dominic.

Dev?

He'd have what he wanted, she told herself. A secure home base for his son. He loves Dominic, and I can help that—nurture it—watch it grow.…

Tick Dev.

The aunts?

I don't know the aunts, so they'd have to come here before any decision's made. It seems ridiculous that two elderly aunts would enjoy this isolated existence, but Dev seems sure. I'd have to meet them, but if he's right…

Tick the aunts.

Tick Lucy. She'd be happy as long as she had Grandpa and a good walk a day. Tick the goats. They'd probably love the aunts. Domineering aunts sounded just what Ernestine needed to curb her goatish bossiness. She might even meet her match.

Maggie smiled into the dark but the smile faded. Everyone had a tick except her.

So…

The only thing in the way here is the stupid way my heart feels every time I look at Dev… The way I feel about Dominic is all tied up in the way I feel about his Dad—but I can't help that.

How to stay unemotional…?

Maybe I can get myself a part-time nursing job to keep myself busy, and spend the rest of my time caring for Grandpa and Dom…I could be happy…

Ha! How can I keep myself lust-free and stay in the same house as Dev?

Maybe I can let myself grow fond…

Don't be ridiculous. Fond? Ha! You're in love already. In lust. Only in lust!

But that wasn't true either, she thought miserably. The way he looked at her—smiled at her—sure, there was lust in the way she was feeling, but there was also warmth and caring and…

And things which interfered with all those wonderful ticks.

Maybe…

Maybe I can just try. Maybe the aunts could just come across and see the island and see what they think, she told herself hesitantly, kissing Dominic's soft curls as he drifted into sleep. Maybe I could visit Dev's farm and just see what happens…

Tomorrow…

Tomorrow she could just see…

Lucy had absconded from her bed. Half an hour later, with Dominic sleeping soundly, Maggie returned to her empty bedroom and sighed. She needed a dog to hug if there was any chance of finding sleep tonight, and Lucy had obviously given up on her. She'd be in soaking up the last warmth from the fire…

So was Dev. Dev was right where she'd left him hours ago, still staring sightlessly into a dying fire, with Lucy curled up beside him. Lucy didn't stir, but Dev looked up as she appeared in the door. He rose and came towards her, but she backed off fast.

'I…I was looking for Lucy. I didn't think you'd still be up.'

'I couldn't sleep if I went to bed,' he said slowly, staring at the girl before him as if he was looking at a ghost.

'Me either.' She took a deep breath. If it was ever to be said, it might as well be said now. There would never be an easier time. 'Dev, I've been thinking.'

He hardly seemed to be listening. He was staring at this wisp of a girl, her long floating nightgown, her tumbling curls, her bare toes and her huge, wondering eyes…

'Maggie, you're beautiful,' he said softly, and she backed further.

'No.'

'No?'

'You bring sex into this in any way, shape or form and it'll mess everything up,' she faltered. 'I mean it.'

He nodded, his eyes not leaving hers. 'So what were you thinking, then, Maggie?'

'I…I just wanted to say that I'll try.'

'Try?'

'Your marriage idea. No!' She snapped the word as once more he stepped closer. His eyes narrowed.

'Maggie?'

'Don't come near me. I don't want you to.' She took a deep breath. 'But…like you said, it could be a sensible decision. As long as you…leave me be. Leave me independent.

'But…'

'Dev, all I'm saying at the moment is that I'm prepared to think about a partnership. About marriage.' She took another jagged breath. 'I think…Dominic's just lovely. He's the dearest little boy and it would give me real pleasure to look after him. But, like you, I see he doesn't need a nanny. He needs a mother.'

'So…'

'And you might be right about Grandpa. He might be as happy off the island as here, as long as he can take Lucy and he has open spaces…'

'My property's a farmlet…'

'And me…' she went on, as if she had to rush before he interrupted. 'I love this island, but I get lonely…'

'I can understand that…'

'So give us time,' she said flatly. 'I'm not rushing into anything, Dev, least of all marriage to someone I've known less than a week. I want references…'

'References?'

'Yes, references. After all, you're applying for a job.'

'What, as your husband?' he asked, startled.

'Yes. It's a business proposition, and that's how I'm treating it. I made my last marriage for emotional reasons. This marriage—if I decide to go ahead—I'm making with my head. And I want to know…'

'What do you want to know?'

'What happens if we marry and then you meet some-one…someone you love?'

'I haven't met anyone in thirty-four years,' he said stead-ily, but even as he said it he knew it was untrue. He'd met her now!

'I guess…you could have an affair,' Maggie said dubi-ously, thinking it through. Dev having an affair? No! But then, if she wasn't offering sex…

'I won't…'

'Don't say it. You can't make promises like that. Not when…' She faltered to a halt. This conversation was im-possible.

'I…need to meet the aunts,' she said at last, after the silence had stretched to a crazy length. 'If the aunts come and like this place—and heaven knows why they would—then maybe we…Grandpa, Dom, you and I…can go to your property on the mainland and check it out. If things still seem okay—seem sensible—then I'll do it.'

'You'll marry me?'

'Yes. But I want guarantees.'

'Guarantees?' His face was closed, guarded, carefully emotionless. 'What sort of guarantees, Maggie?'

'Independence, mostly,' she said, wiggling her bare feet on the floor and wishing she'd put something more formal on than her nightie. She needed a business suit here. And a couple of accountants taking notes! 'I'll agree to be there for Dominic outside school hours, though I'll expect you to do the same as much as possible, and I'll care for Grandpa. But there's no way you're running my life. If I want to take a part-time job…make friends outside our marriage…control my own money….'

'Then you'll do it,' he said, staring down in concern at

the note of anguish in the voice she was trying so hard to keep business-like. 'Maggie, that's what marriage is.'

'Not in my experience it's not. And bedrooms…' She took a deep breath. 'I want separate bedrooms. I meant what I said about not minding about you having affairs, but not with me. No sex, Devlin. I don't want sex.'

'You're kidding!' The exclamation was impossible to suppress, and Dev watched as Maggie's colour mounted to crimson.

'I don't!'

'No. Well…' Somehow he hauled himself back under control, pushing away the thought of her reaction up in the lighthouse. If he took her any further down that road she'd run, and he had the sense to know it. Too much was at stake here to press his point. 'That's fine,' he agreed gently. 'I've told you—I'm not in the market for a relationship.'

'It's important, Dev. You need to understand that there's no way I want a real marriage—in any sense of the word. I still feel married to Michael.'

'You mean you still feel guilty?'

'Whatever,' she said wretchedly. 'But if you think it can work… Dev, we could try.'

'Try marriage?'

'No.' Her face shuttered down in a barrier—excluding him solidly. 'You don't *try* marriage. If I make vows, then I keep them. I mean try the arrangements. Get…get to know each other a bit better. Maybe have a week at your home and leave the aunts here—then come back and think about it. See if we can keep things platonic and business-like, but make a warm home for Dom and Grandpa…'

This whole proposition was starting to sound crazy, Dev decided as he watched her anguished face. When he'd first thought of it, his plan had seemed like the wonderful solution to all their problems, but the more Dev looked at this waif-like girl/woman the crazier it now seemed.

Marriage, but not a marriage…

It had seemed so sensible as a business plan, but now, standing in the dim light with Maggie before him, her eyes pleading…

'Okay, Maggie, we'll try it,' he said heavily, and heaven knew what effort it cost him to stay right where he was—to fail to take her into his arms right there and then. Lord knew he wanted to.

Business? Was that what he'd thought this was? Yeah, maybe, but he hadn't counted on her absolute loveliness…loveliness in a form that made his gut wrench…

Maybe one day, when the ghost of Michael was finally laid to rest, and when the pain and guilt had faded in the warmth of what they could build…

Yeah. One day some semblance of a real marriage might be possible—if he could keep his hands off her in the meantime.

He looked across the room at her and for the first time in years the thought of marriage stirred him—marriage as it really could be. She'd offered to let him have affairs. Ha! What man would want an affair with this woman in his home? This woman in his arms.

This woman responding as he knew she could.

But if he moved now…if he tried to warm the fires lying dormant in her, then she'd run a mile. She was like a wild and wounded thing. Her trust was there to be gained, but first…first she had to heal.

Good grief! What a time to realise he wanted more than a marriage of convenience. He wanted Maggie.

Tread carefully, Macafferty, he told himself harshly. Tread carefully. Because what you're fighting for is growing more precious by the minute. It might take years…but it might just be worth being patient.

So… 'It's a business proposition, Maggie,' he said softly. 'A sensible, considered proposition between two people who need each other. Let's take it as that. Yeah, I'll give you references, but I can tell you now that there's no need. You can trust me. I won't come near you—unless you want—and if you like, then you can have that written into the wedding vows.'

Unless you want…

The words hung between them and Maggie's eyes widened. She hadn't expected that—but as a promise she couldn't ask for more.

And it was fine, she thought wildly. To not come near her unless she wanted… Well, that was fine because she didn't want.

Did she?

'That's okay, then, Dev,' she managed, and somehow she kept her voice calm. 'Agreed.'

Then she turned and fled down the passage before he could read the gamut of emotions running across her face. Because calm was the last thing this man made her feel.

The airline strike lifted two days later, and twelve hours after that the aunts arrived by chartered helicopter. They climbed off the helicopter onto the island, two demure, white-haired old ladies, dressed in sensible tweed skirts, cardigans and stout shoes, and looking for all the world like women who could be anyone's grandmas.

That impression lasted a whole two seconds—long enough for the first lady to open her mouth.

Dev and Dominic and Maggie had walked over to the plateau on the far side of the island to meet them. Dev stepped forward and was met head-on by his aunt Molly.

'Devlin.' His shoulders were gripped by two wrinkled hands, his cheek was given a perfunctory peck and then he was shaken. Firmly. Five foot two of white-haired old lady shaking six feet two of strongly built male, and doing it with force.

'For heaven's sake, we were so worried about you and the little boy,' she burst out, and for an astounded moment Maggie thought Dev's ears were going to be boxed. 'What were you thinking of? Fancy hiring a chartered plane—heavens, you don't know who could have used one of those nasty things before you got to it, and goodness knows what state the engine was in. You were lucky you weren't killed. Mr Scott here —' a finger was pointed back at the hapless helicopter pilot '—very kindly supplied us with copies of all his credentials *and* his service logs before we flew, but Myrtle said we shouldn't come until we checked it out for ourselves so she's been all over the engine, and that's what you should have done.'

'Myrtle's been inspecting the helicopter engine?' Dev said faintly, rolling his eyes at the unfortunate pilot.

'Yes, dear. You know she learned to fly when she was running the cattle station, and we've both always said—ever since our dear father put us on the back of a horse and gave us this very good advice—that you don't ride what you don't know. It's held us in very good stead, and it would have helped you, too, if you'd been sensible. Now... Is this indeed Dominic? And is this the Maggie we've been hearing about?'

Molly's sister Myrtle had reached her side now—she'd been at a disadvantage in having to come around the helicopter to reach them—but now the two elderly women stood side by side and stared, summing Dominic and Maggie from the toes up.

'Goodness,' Myrtle said. 'Isn't Dominic like you?'

'Goodness,' Molly said. 'Isn't Maggie pretty?'

Then their eyes left the people and roved—taking in every inch of the island they could see. Maggie watched, stunned. She could almost see anticipation shining brightly in their minds.

'This sounds a very good idea, Devlin,' Myrtle said at last. 'A cheese factory, you said. And kelp… I started reading up on kelp the minute your radio call came through, and there's uses for more types of kelp than bull kelp. No offence, Maggie dear, but if you're going to collect it then you should maximise your profit. I've rung pharmaceutical companies worldwide and I have lists of every type of kelp we can sell. Plus we spent yesterday at the university's botany department, with a very knowledgeable marine biologist—I'm sure we can now identify everything we're looking for.'

'And the cheese…' Molly broke in. 'Maggie, did you know your outlets mark your cheese up by a hundred per cent, on the basis that it's perishable and they won't sell it all—but they do. Everything you supply is snapped up. We've been right into it. If we take over, we'll keep your quality, of course, but there's no sense in letting middle men take all your profits. That sort of profit should come back into the business.'

'I didn't know…' Maggie started, but Molly shook her head.

'No, but we do, dear, and if there's one thing we're good at it's driving a bargain. Devlin, I think we should see the goats straight away.'

'You don't need to,' Maggie said faintly, and then she paused. The goats had scattered with the noise of the helicopter, but they'd only moved back as far as was necessary. Maggie had expected them to come forward now, as the rotors slowed to silence.

Instead, she looked behind her and saw a mass of hooves scattering away to the other side of the island.

She had to grin. Ernestine had clearly met her match, and it was a wise goat who knew when to retreat.

By the end of the following day it was Maggie who felt like retreating. Put simply, her life had been overwhelmed. She had nothing to do. Every time she started something, an aunt was at her elbow, demanding instruction, taking it on board with fierce intelligence and then taking over to the manner born. Any doubts as to the aunts' ability to cope were soon replaced by doubts as to whether the two redoubtable old ladies would find enough to do.

'Well, we mightn't,' Molly admitted. 'But we've thought of that. What do you say to us taking on paying guests?'

'Paying…?'

'Now, it's a partnership,' Myrtle interrupted. 'The lease is in your grandfather's name, so it's his decision—but you have to agree the house won't stand much longer without attention. Molly and I have been talking. We thought if you agreed, and if this trial works out, then we'll sink some of our retirement funds into restoring the house—then take exclusive house guests. Two at a time. Charge them a bomb. Let them milk a goat or two if they behave themselves. What do you think?'

Maggie opened her mouth to protest, but she wasn't given the chance.

'It's a damned good idea,' Joe said solidly from his seat on a stone bench in the sun. 'Hannah and I would have liked to do that if we'd been a bit more prosperous. I can show you the plans Hannah drew up, if you like.'

The aunts and Grandpa went off into the house in a threesome huddle, and Maggie stared at their retreating backs in astonishment. This wasn't her island, she told herself. The island was leased to Joe. And somehow, in all their planning, he'd been given his independence again. It was he making the decisions. Not Maggie.

She should be rapt. This was what she wanted—wasn't it? Joe could come to the mainland with Maggie and then return to his island to see his plans in action whenever he wished.

She turned to find Dev watching her. They'd been sitting on the rock ledge at the front of the house. Now, with oldies gone inside, and with Dom throwing sticks into the water for Lucy to bring back, they were alone.

'It looks like it's working, Maggie,' Dev said softly, and Maggie flushed.

'I…yes…'

'Doesn't that make you happy?'

'I guess it must.' She twisted the ring on her finger and Dev saw, leaned over and caught her hand in both of his.

'Maggie, this is not betraying Michael.'

'I never thought it was. It's only…'

'Only what?'

'It's happening too fast.'

'It can't happen fast enough for five of us.'

'You…?' She looked up and met his steady gaze. 'You really do want us to be married?'

There was only one way to answer that, and Dev answered with his heart.

'Yes, Maggie, I do.'

'Why?' She tilted her chin and met his gaze. 'It's not just for Dom—is it?'

'No,' he agreed, and he released her hand. The link between them was chafing her—he could see that. There was tension written in every line on her face.

'Why, then?'

He shrugged, and tried a smile. The smile made his eyes

dance and Maggie felt her heart twist—which made her feel even worse. Heck, she didn't want any heart-twisting. It scared her stupid!

'I couldn't just ask anyone to be a mother to my son,' he said gently. 'It would have to be a pretty special lady to be that—and that's pretty much how I'm feeling. The more I get to know you, the more special you feel to me.'

'Dev…'

'I know you don't want it, but there it is. I'm your friend, Maggie, and I want to be your husband. I told you—I won't push further than that unless you want it.'

'It won't work,' she whispered.

'I don't see why not. Unless you intend your guilt to stand in the way of your future. Of our future…'

'You make it sound like my guilt is something I have control over.'

'Maybe it is. Maybe you should get angry—let it out…'

'See a therapist?' she said mockingly. 'Why? So I'll fall into bed with you?'

'That's not fair, Maggie,' he said, and once more he reached out to touch her.

'N…no.' She pulled her hand away and rose to stand looking out to sea. 'I'm sorry. I guess…it's just that it's so perfect for everyone, and I hardly seem to have had time to think, and now…tomorrow we're leaving.'

'Only for a week, Maggie. The agreement is to leave the aunts here for a week, and for us to try out Hobart. And then we come back here to make a choice.'

'I think choices are already being made.' There was a whoop of laughter from inside the house and Joe's chuckle rang out. Joe was in his element. Maggie hadn't seen him so happy since before Hannah died—and she couldn't interfere with anything that made him happy.

Another pressure…

'Maggie, we all have to be happy about this—you included. There's no way you're being blackmailed into anything.' Dev's smile died and his voice grew stern. 'There's been enough blackmail for you in the past to last a lifetime.'

'I…' Maggie shook her head. 'Dev, I'm going to milk the goats.' She was out of her depth here and she had the sense to know it. 'Will you tell the aunts I'm doing it alone tonight?'

'You want to be by yourself?'

'Yes,' she said shortly, but Dom was swinging away from Lucy and rushing to her side.

'Being by yourself doesn't mean me, does it, Maggie?' he asked urgently. 'I can come? Lucy and I can come?'

The claustrophobia was still there, but Maggie looked down at Dom's pleading face and knew isolation, for her, was a thing of the past.

'Yes, Dom, you can come.'

'Because being by yourself means just being with Dad and me now—doesn't it?' he said, and Maggie swallowed her fears and nodded.

'And with Grandpa and Lucy. Yes, Dom, I guess—from now on—that it does.'

CHAPTER EIGHT

JOE didn't come with them to the mainland. He was enjoying himself too darned much where he was, and when the supply boat arrived to collect them he dug in his toes and stayed put.

'I'll come if I need to, but it's you who has to do the deciding, Maggie love, and Molly and Myrtle reckon they can look after me as well as they can the goats.'

They could. There was no way Maggie could deny it. But it didn't stop a lump forming in the back of her throat as she waved goodbye to her island and her grandfather—and her isolation.

She was being transported from one life to another, but the choice was increasingly out of her hands.

'He'll come to us eventually,' Dev said, standing at the boat rail and watching the receding island with her. He guessed she was thinking of Joe. 'Just not yet. He's having too good a time. Now it's up to us to do the same—have a really good time ourselves. It's only a week's trial, but let's see just how good we can make it, Maggie.'

'Mmm.' Still her heart was filled with doubts, but she managed a smile. The day was lovely, the sea was millpond-smooth and the soft sea breeze was ruffling her hair. She was on her way to the possibility of a new life.

She was terrified!

First stop in Hobart was a computer shop, and Dominic was almost beside himself with joy.

'You choose,' Dev told his son, then calmly sat back and

watched. Every time the salesman turned to him he simply shook his head, as if he didn't understand what the salesman was saying. 'Ask my son,' he told the man. 'Dominic, tell Mr Roberts exactly what you need.'

Dominic looked from Maggie to Dev, as if unable to believe his eyes—and then he turned back to the salesman.

'I can choose by myself.' It was as if he was telling himself as well as the salesman, and the salesman beamed.

'You can indeed,' he agreed. 'You're a very lucky boy to have such a generous mum and dad.'

Dominic swallowed, and glanced back at Maggie. Then he took a deep breath and puffed his chest out like a turkey cock.

'Yes, I am,' he announced. 'Can I get a computer with *Flight Warrior* on it? And the internet?'

Of course he could, and he walked out of the shop clutching his new laptop computer and looking proud fit to burst. But…

'You know what was the best thing about buying my new computer?' he confided to his adults as he walked back to Dev's car—they'd collected it from where it had sat for a week at the airport.

'What was the best thing, Dominic?' Maggie asked, and the lump in her throat was getting bigger.

'He thought I had a real mum and dad,' Dom said. 'Just like other kids.'

Yeah, right. The lump was threatening to choke her.

And then there was the ride out to Dev's farmlet, five miles out of the city. Farmlet? Dev might call it a farmlet but it looked like a real farm to Maggie. It was beautiful, lush and green with ancient trees, gnarled and twisted by the years, scattered over undulating paddocks. The place whispered peace—the only sign of life being the clusters of rusty red Hereford cattle grazing peacefully in the sun.

The house was old and graceful, made of stone with a low-slung verandah all around. A rose-covered arch spanned a wide cattle grid separating the garden from the farm, and beyond the arch there seemed nothing but roses.

'It's beautiful,' Maggie gasped, and Dev turned to her and smiled.

'So you have a voice. I was beginning to think you two had lost your tongues entirely.'

It was true that they'd been silent. Dom had sat in the back seat and cradled his computer and beamed all the way from town—and Maggie...well, she'd grown more and more quiet the closer she'd grown to Dev's property. Dev's domain...

'I'm sorry,' she managed.

'Don't be.' He leaned across and took her hand in his, and his eyes smiled a caress all by themselves. 'Welcome to Bunyoonda. Welcome to the place I hope you can call your home.'

Then, before he could see the look of strain flash across her face, his attention was diverted. A middle-aged lady had appeared on the front verandah, stout, aproned and beaming a smile a mile wide.

'Mrs Collins,' Dev breathed. 'Thank you, Lord...'

'Who...?' Maggie followed his gaze, puzzled.

'When the aunts decided to retire to look after me, they hadn't expected me to already be looked after. They thought I should put Mrs Collins out to pasture—which I refused to do. She's been my housekeeper for years. However...when I left to fetch Dominic she was threatening to quit. And now...'

'Now you have your nice ordered life back together

again,' Maggie said softly, and it was impossible to keep the note of bitterness from her voice.

'Yes, I have,' Dev said gently, turning to face her. He smiled. 'I've been incredibly lucky.'

'I guess…'

'Maggie, it will work…'

'Because you want it to.'

'So do you.'

'I don't know…'

But there was no time to think now. There was the sound of hysterical barking and three dogs burst around the side of the house—followed by four black and white puppies, tumbling over themselves in their eagerness to join their mother.

'Well, well…' Dev grinned. 'Silky's puppies have found their legs.'

'Puppies…' Dom gasped, staring from the car window in stunned amazement, his beam threatening to split his face. 'You have four puppies.'

'One of them can be yours,' Dev told him, opening the car door and bracing himself for the onslaught of dogs. 'You just have to choose. What do you think of your new home, Dominic?'

'It's ace,' Dominic breathed, and when he tumbled from the car in his eagerness to reach the pups, he even left his new computer sitting on the back seat.

And Maggie? Dev came around to help her from the car, and for some stupid reason she needed help—her legs had turned to jelly.

'Do you think it might be ace, too, Maggie?' Dev asked, as he took her hand and led her up the verandah to meet Mrs Collins. 'Do you reckon?'

'I don't reckon anything,' Maggie said weakly. 'I…I'll just have to wait and see.'

*   *   *

If she'd ever indulged in the idea of being a kept woman, this would be kept woman heaven, Maggie thought bleakly. She sat on the bank of the creek down from the house, watching Dominic fish for yabbies, and she felt the familiar pangs of claustrophobia grow worse by the minute.

This was lovely, she told herself, so how on earth could she complain? The sun was on her face, there were puppies playing at her feet, and Dominic had caught three large yabbies—or maybe he'd caught the same yabby three times. Dev had decreed school could wait. A term's break wouldn't hurt his son's chances in life, and he needed settling time.

Joe had radioed the night before, and there had been no mistaking his pleasure in the way his life had changed. The aunts were coping brilliantly and Maggie was very welcome to stay exactly where she was. They were happy.

So was Dominic. He'd hardly had time for his computer the whole time he'd been at the farm. He retired occasionally for short bursts of computer comfort—almost as if he needed breathing space from these amazing new relationships he was forging—but he re-emerged to greet his friends with joy.

His friends. His new puppy, Wobble. Mrs Collins, who made the best chocolate cake Dominic had ever eaten and knew exactly what small boys liked to eat. And Maggie—and there was no doubt as to the role he'd assigned her. Mum… It was only a matter of time before he came right out and called her that.

And Dev?

Devlin of the business hours.

That was part of the problem, Maggie thought bitterly, Maybe it was why she felt so damned claustrophobic. Dev had pressing business needs that took him away at eight each morning and saw him come home after five. Dominic of the many-fathers-in-the-past knew this pattern, and accepted it, finding pleasure in the time he did spend with Dev, but Maggie was not so sure.

Working father with housewife mother?

Yeah, right…

Dev said he wanted a wife, and he looked at her with eyes that were filled with warmth and also with desire. If she raised a finger she'd be in his bed, she knew, and the contract would be complete. Happiness for everyone…

'Penny for them?'

She jumped about a foot, and when she came back to land Dev was sinking down on the bank beside her.

'What…?'

'I finished work early,' he said in a smug tone. 'So I came home to see what my family were doing.'

Keeping tabs on the little woman…

'We're yabbying,' she said, and her voice was strained.

'Hey, I guessed that.' He motioned to the nets. 'Where's the catch?'

'We work on a catch and release system,' Maggie told him, trying to keep her voice even. 'We intend to grow monsters in this creek. We'll catch them year after year, and watch them grow, and we can't do that if we eat them.'

'Hey, I like eating yabbies,' Dev said, aggrieved, but Maggie shook her head.

'Find your own creek, then. This is ours.'

'That's possessive.'

'Yes.' Damn, her voice was breathless again.

'Maggie?'

'Yes?'

'Come out to dinner with me.'

'What…?'

'You heard. Dinner. This evening.' He smiled, that blazingly attractive smile that made her heart stand still. It was a smile that could persuade her to do anything, she thought helplessly, and he kept right on persuading. 'Dom's been awake since the crack of dawn—he did the rounds of the cattle with me before I went to work—so he'll be out like a light by eight. Mrs Collins will take care of him. The evening's ours.'

'Dev…'

'Maggie.'

'I don't know…'

'Maggie, our week's trial should have some time kept free for us,' he said lightly—but there was nothing light in the way he was looking at her. His eyes were on hers, warm and sure and compelling.

'I don't know whether it's wise.'

'Meaning you want this kept as a business bargain?'

'Yes.'

He nodded, his eyes still watchful. 'Then come out to dinner and talk business with me,' he told her. 'There are things to discuss. I need to fly to New York in the morning.'

'New York…' Her eyes flew wide in dismay. 'But our week…'

'I'm sorry, he said apologetically. 'But it can't be helped. With the fall in the dollar, we're having to restructure our company's finances.' His smile intensified. 'It's okay, though, Maggie. I'm not going broke. I don't like leaving Dominic so soon, but he'll understand and it's not as though I'm leaving him alone. I'm leaving him with you.'

'Very convenient.' She couldn't keep the waspishness from her voice, and his smile widened even further. Honestly, if he knew how close she was to slapping that smug look right from his face…

'It's part of the bargain,' Dev said patiently. 'This is how it will be. I need to travel. Dom needs a stable base.'

'And I'm it.'

'You're it.' He leaned over and kissed her on the nose. 'And a very lovely stable base you are, too, dearest Maggie.'

'Doormat Maggie!' she snapped. 'And this trial was only supposed to be for a week.' She wiped her nose, as if she was wiping off a grubby smudge, but his smile still didn't fade. The man was maddening!

'You're not a doormat, and I know it's only for a week, but I'll be back on Friday, in time to take you back to the island. If you wish. But...do you wish, Maggie?'

'I...'

'You couldn't be happy here long-term?'

Maggie caught her breath. She stared helplessly at Dev as her past came rushing back. A vision of Michael flooded into her head: Michael standing in the living room of his fabulous mansion and gesturing around them—at plush carpets and leather lounge suites and furnishings that screamed money from every angle.

'I don't see why you can't be happy here,' he'd complained, when she'd insisted on working. 'You don't need anything else but what's between these four walls...'

What was Dev doing? Saying the same? Was it her fate to be a permanently kept woman?

Dev saw the expression on her face, and his smile finally died.

'Hey, Maggie, let's not get our knickers in a knot here,' he said gently. 'The out is always yours at the end of the week. I promised you that, and I meant it.'

'I know.' But it wasn't that easy, she thought helplessly. It was more than Devlin keeping her here now, and he knew it.

But he was still in persuasion mode. 'Let's just go out to dinner and enjoy ourselves,' he said. 'Maggie, if you decide to go back to the island on Saturday, then this may be our only chance.'

'Yeah.' She took a deep breath. Right.

'Do we have a date?'

She looked up at him, and it was impossible not to smile at the man. Not when he had that endearing, cocker spaniel look of innocence in his eyes, even when she knew the innocence was totally deceiving. Not when he looked like…like Devlin.

'Yeah, all right,' she said ungraciously. 'We have a date.'

'Best restaurant in Hobart,' he said, beaming his very best cocker spaniel smile. If he'd had a tail, it would have wagged. 'And dancing. Wear your best, Maggie.'

'I…I'll do it, but…maybe I'll think of this as our farewell dinner, then,' she said uncertainly. 'Dev, that's the only reason I'm agreeing to this.'

His smile died again, and he looked at her for a long, long minute.

'There's a long time until Saturday,' he told her at last. 'There's a lot of thinking to be done before then,' He smiled again, more gently this time. 'Keep thinking, Maggie. There's no decisions to be made just yet.'

He touched her oh, so lightly on the cheek—and then he went to help his son and heir catch yabbies.

Maggie spent a heap of time deciding what to wear. In the end she decided she hated everything. Apart from her jeans and her homespun skirt and shawl, every single thing she wore screamed Michael. He'd been with her when she chose them. Or rather, she'd been present when Michael had chosen them. They were Michael's clothes—not hers.

Black and white. Black and white… No colour. Michael had hated colour.

In the end she pulled on a little black dress—safe, conservative and chic. It was cut low at the back, but its breast-line was demure and it almost reached her knees.

Black… She hated it even more than white.

It couldn't matter. She had to be sensible here—so she brushed her hair up into the stylish knot Michael had decreed went with the dress, pulled on sheer nylons and slipped on black stilettoes—and then she stared in the mirror for a very long time. This was the Maggie that Michael had wanted to possess utterly—and she hated her.

Go on, Maggie, she told herself crossly. You're being silly. Wearing this is the sensible thing to do. Be nice to the man. It's only until Saturday.

But the fine webs of commitment were drawing closer. And Maggie's needs were somehow behind everyone else's…

She had to go out to the sitting room some time. When she did, Dev was waiting, and, as he unwound his long body from the settee, she swallowed a gasp. Up until now she'd only seen him in casuals. Dressed in a deep black dinner suit, he looked so handsome he almost took her breath away.

Just like Michael…

But he was watching her face, and he saw…

'Maggie, what's the trouble?'

'Nothing,' she said shortly. 'Let's go.'

'You look lovely,' he said, puzzled. His eyes didn't leave her face. 'That dress is stunning.'

'Yes. I know. Michael chose it.'

His face cleared. He understood. 'Why the hell are you wearing it, then?' he demanded. 'I hate it. Take it off immediately.'

'I don't have anything else to wear except the clothes

Michael chose.' She shrugged. 'That's all I own. Come on. I'm being stupid.'

'If I'd known, I could have picked you up something in town today.'

'Sure,' she said dully. 'Dressed by Devlin instead of dressed by Michael. It's all the same. Let's leave. I'm sure these clothes are elegant enough to fit expectations. I won't shame you.'

'Maggie…'

'What?'

'Turn around.'

She frowned. 'Why?'

For answer he took her shoulders and turned her forcibly away from him. Then, before she could stop him, he lifted the zip fastener at her back—and pulled it down, with such force that it ripped right down to the hem.

The dress parted.

'Oh, heck,' Dev said sadly, turning her around again so she was vaguely decent and her astounded gaze met his. 'Don't worry, love. I'm not intent on anything indecent here—more's the pity—but your dress is ruined. Go and put something on that *you* choose.'

'I don't…' She could hardly believe what he'd just done. 'Dev…how dare you! I don't own anything else.'

'What about your homespun?'

Maggie gasped. 'Don't be silly. You can't take me out in my homespun.'

'I'd take you out stark naked, Maggie,' he said softly, and his finger traced the line of her cheek. 'I swear. You're lovely. The loveliest thing. But it's not your dresses that are important to me. It's you.'

She gasped again. 'Dev…'

'I know, I'm not supposed to say it,' he told her. 'But it's there, and it's growing. Go and put your homespun skirt on, Maggie. I want to take you out. *You.* Not some dressed up doll that Michael orchestrated. I want you as you really are.'

She was crazy to be anywhere near this man, she decided, as she hauled off her ruined dress and slipped on her home-spun skirt. He called her fey, but it was he who was casting a spell.

She pulled the combs from her hair and let her curls hang free, then slid golden hoops into her ears and stared at her reflection in indecision. Michael would never have let her out of the house looking like this. In her soft blouse, with her flowing skirt and her lovely multicoloured shawl, she looked part-gypsy, part-hippy, part...

'Maggie...' she said aloud. 'I'm Maggie. No one else. And I'm going to dinner with Dev...'

Dev... Her voice fell to silence at the sound of his name. Dev... Lord, why was she so afraid?

Without her chic image, she'd half expected Dev to change his mind about where he was taking her—maybe fish and chips on the river bank would be more appropriate—but when she walked back into the living room, she found he was still wearing his dinner suit, and still waiting to take her just where he'd first intended.

'Don't worry about it,' he growled when she demurred. 'You look better than any woman I've ever seen. No quibbles.'

'But...'

'*But's* a quibble. I'm not listening.'

There was nothing for it. She shut up and didn't quibble at all, or at least, not out loud...

The restaurant was the last word in elegance—the sort of place Michael had loved, and definitely the sort of place

that screamed for a little black dress. Maggie walked in the
door and almost regretted changing. She felt like a fish out
of water in her crazy clothes—but the waiter appeared not
to notice that they were inappropriate. How could he in the
face of Dev's attitude?

'This is Maggie,' Dev told him as they were ushered to
their table, and there was such a note of pride in his voice
that anyone criticising the girl on his arm could expect to
be slugged.

Her doubts faded in the face of his pride. Good grief! It
was all Maggie could do not to grin as she made her way
through the sophisticated diners, and the tone of Dev's
voice made her tilt her chin and carry the thing off
with style. If Dev sounded proud of her, surely she
couldn't…what had he said? Quibble?

So she swept past the rest of the black-clad diners—her
crimson skirt brushing the floor—and when they were
seated at what surely had to be the best table in the house
she chuckled.

'What's the joke?'

'They're all wondering where you got the crazy lady,'
she told him. 'And figuring that the circus is in town.'

'Nope. They're all wishing they'd worn their crimson,'
Dev said serenely. 'And the men are wondering why their
women aren't wearing wonderful clothes like yours.'

'Yeah?'

'Yeah. Definitely yeah. Start with champagne, Maggie. I
want this to be a very special night.'

It was a *very* special night, but it had nothing to do with
the champagne. It had to do with the way Dev smiled at
her—the warmth of the approval in his eyes—the way his
fingers touched hers as they talked.

They were like a long-married couple, Maggie thought

wonderingly as the night wore on, with child, aunts, grand-parent, dogs, housekeeper, home to talk of. Dev talked, listened, smiled—and not once did his attention stray from her.

He was so different from Michael...

Where Michael would have been looking about the res-taurant, seeing how they compared to other couples, Dev seemed not to care. He had eyes only for her—and as a seduction technique it worked a treat. By the time coffee arrived that was exactly how she was feeling. As if she was in the middle of practised seduction—and enjoying it very, very much.

'Liqueur?' he asked, and Maggie shook her head. The champagne had gone right to her head and stayed there—or something had.

'No.'

'Afraid?' There was a twinkle lurking behind his eyes and Maggie drew in her breath.

'What on earth would I have to be afraid of?'

'Maybe yourself.'

'And what's that supposed to mean?'

'Nothing.' He grinned and held up his hands placatingly. 'Not a thing, Maggie love, or at least not a thing I can explain to you. It's only something you can explain to your-self. Let's go home.'

Maggie love... Home...

The thought made Maggie almost unable to breathe. Home... With Dev.

They'd been silent on the journey into Hobart, and they were even more silent going home. Dev's powerful Jaguar cut through the night in hushed comfort, and Maggie hugged her knees, stared straight ahead and wished des-perately—for what?

She needed something like Dr Who's telephone box, she decided at last—something to transport her instantly from one world to another. To take her back to her island, her stark little bedroom and her isolation.

To a life where things were safe—because things weren't safe here.

She cast a sideways look at Dev and looked away just as fast. He'd been talkative all night, keeping her chuckling and happy, but now... He'd hardly drunk anything, he looked tired, and tomorrow he was heading to New York.

It was he who was being transported to another world, she thought. Not she. And when he came home from New York... Would she be waiting for him?

'Maggie, this marriage we're talking of is not a death sentence,' he said softly, still concentrating on his driving, and Maggie's breath drew in as a startled gasp. He knew what she was thinking.

'I wasn't... I never said...'

'There's no drama if you want to go back to your island.'

'No.'

'We'll all survive without you.'

'Yes.'

Dev turned the car into the homestead gate, pulled to a halt and turned to her. 'Maggie, let me be clear,' he said, and his voice was firm. 'I'm holding no gun to your head. Dominic thinks you're here as a friend. He might talk of wanting you as a mother, but he knows you're not. I'd like you to continue as his friend. I think that's important—the more constants he has in his life now the better—but you're not to talk yourself into marriage solely because of Dominic.'

'I...'

'Or Joe,' he went on ruthlessly. 'You'll not marry because of Joe—or Molly or Myrtle or Lucy or Ernestine.

Sure, they'd all be happy if you married me, but they'll survive and be happy if you don't. Even I...'

He paused, then let go the wheel, but stayed staring out into the night. The firmness in his voice turned to absolute steel. 'Even I would survive. I don't say I'd be happy, but I'd survive. There's no gun to your head.'

'Dev...'

'But...if you marry me, then I would be happy,' he went on heavily. 'I'm beginning to think...sod the business arrangement. If you marry me it had better be for you. Because it would make you happy. I'm starting to think I don't want you under any other terms.'

'Dev, you said...'

'I said it could be a business arrangement,' he told her. 'I was stupid. You've been in my house for two days, and I no longer think any business arrangement is on the cards. I've tried to keep it like that but it isn't possible. I want you.'

Silence. The silence went on, unending and powerful. Maggie knotted her fingers and stared down at them in the moonlight, trying desperately to find words...to find a reply.

There was none to give.

Finally Dev swore. 'I'm sorry, Maggie,' he said gently. 'I know it's too soon. I'm an oaf when it comes to relationships. You see, I can't—'

He broke off, then swore again, shoved open his car door and came around to help his lady alight. She rose, brushed against him as she passed, and took two steps away. Then she paused. And looked back...

He was still standing by the car, his hand on the open door. The smell of roses hung heavily in the air. The moonlight was on his face, accentuating the lean, sculpted lines—the harsh marring of the scar across his forehead.

He was an oaf when it came to relationships, he said. Dear heaven…

She'd thought he was the strong one, but now…in the moonlight…he looked vulnerable and alone, and she knew he was capable of as much hurt as she was. Dev…

Maggie stood, uncertain, while her heart twisted within.

Don't! her mind was screaming. Don't let this man near to you. You've been down this road before. He'll hold you…use you…if you give it to him, then he'll break your heart…

It was too late. He was looking at her with that dear uncertainty playing across his face. He wouldn't push her, she knew. Honourable fool…

Beloved fool.

Her heart was knotting in pain—in indecision—but suddenly the uncertainty ceased. The knot unravelled as if someone had slipped the ends, so the knot was simply a fine line—an arrow pointing in one direction.

The future lay before her, in the uncertainty she saw on Dev's face. She knew, suddenly, that whatever danger lay ahead, whatever tomorrow held, tonight had its own sweet destiny.

Tonight was Dev. It must be.

It was.

She closed her eyes, and when she opened them she knew what she must do. She took one deep, steadying breath—and then she walked two steps back to where he waited. She put her hands up to hold his face between her palms—and then she stood on tiptoes and she kissed him.

For one long moment he stood rigid in the sheer unexpectedness of it. No matter. She kissed him again, full on the lips, because there was no way she was changing her mind now. No way!

'Maggie…' His voice was a hoarse whisper, drowned in

her second kiss. She felt his shock at her capitulation and then she felt his joy. It flowed straight through his body—she felt it like a bolt of lightning—and then it was returned, renewed, strengthened and given back in full. His hands came around her waist and she was gathered to him...

And in that moment, she was his!

'Maggie...'

His body was steel against hers. There was no going back now. He gave a low moan of triumph—of joy. Her breasts were crushed to his chest and her feet were lifted off the ground as he claimed her for his own. She felt herself whisper a moan of pleasure as wave after wave of desire coursed through her.

There was nothing else in the world apart from this man.

Dev was her world. For tonight...for this moment...this man was her beloved. Whatever tomorrow brought—a world of separation—whatever—tonight was theirs and couldn't be gainsaid.

Then she was being lifted with a long, low laugh of conquest, raised into his arms and swept up the verandah through the open French windows to the bedroom beyond. The room was in darkness, but by the faint moonlight Maggie could see the bed, a vast low island in the centre of the room. It was turned back in readiness—as if it had been waiting. As if Dev had been waiting...

Then Dev laid his lady gently down onto the cool linen sheets, and kissed her oh, so tenderly... As if she was the most precious thing in the entire world.

'My love, are you sure?'

'Sure.' It was barely a whisper, but all the love she held was in that word. He smiled down at her, and his smile made her heart stand still.

'Then don't go away,' he said softly. And he rose...

It was as much as she could do not to cry in protest.
Why? Why?

But he was still smiling, that lovely caressing smile that
held her in thrall. That held her to his heart. 'No babies—
at least not tonight,' he told her lovingly. 'Maybe tomorrow…'

Contraception. Of course. She hadn't even thought. Stupid, stupid, stupid—but Michael had had a vasectomy—of
course he had—there had been no way Michael was risking
babies—and she'd stopped fearing something she'd wanted
so much. A child…

But Dev had been burned before. A marriage because of
unplanned pregnancy… Of course he'd be careful.

She barely had time to think this through before he was
back, and she could wait no longer. She was wanton…
Aching… Hungering for her man…

As he walked out from the bathroom door she slid her
blouse from her shoulders, her skirt fell free—and she was
waiting for him…

Heaven was waiting… For each of them.

He was magnificent, and he was sinking to meet her—
to enfold her in his arms. Her skin met his—gloriously—
and the full length of their bodies merged into a mist of
heat and desire and love. Skin against skin. Heart against
heart.

One heart… This was her love. Her heart.

Her home.

And that was the last thing she was capable of thinking
of as the night melted into a fiery glow. Her heart was
ablaze with love. She was where she was meant to be.

One, with her love.

Afterwards, she slept as she hadn't slept for years, cradled
in Dev's strong arms, locked as if he would never let her

go.

His sleep, like hers, was total. It was as if he, too, had found his home. The world was not here. Their love was total. Within each other's arms, the world was kept at bay.

Dawn admitted the world again. There was still the journey to New York, which couldn't be delayed.

'You couldn't come too?' Dev said wistfully, as he kissed her for what surely must be the two thousandth time.

The thought was almost irresistible, but there were things that had to be thought through. Dominic, for one... Somehow she made herself be practical.

'You're flying there and back in four days... That's about forty hours in an aeroplane. No, thank you very much.'

'And they don't have beds in aeroplanes, either.' Dev sighed heavily and pulled her closer. 'Maybe we could take Dom...stay longer...' And then he sighed again. 'Hell, no we can't. I have to be back for the company general meeting next week. What was I thinking of, saying I could stay longer? You're making my mind fuzzy, woman!'

'Mine's completely shot,' she confessed, and he grinned.

'We both sound punch drunk. I've been away from the business for nearly two weeks and I need to concentrate.' He groaned and pulled her closer. 'And now you're making me think just about as clearly as a rabbit caught in headlights.'

Dev, too... That was just how *she* was feeling, Maggie thought hazily. Like a rabbit caught in headlights—lights so powerful she couldn't look away. But...someone had to be sensible.

'Go on.' She gave him a shove away from her. 'Get

yourself into gear. I'm heading back to my room before Dominic wakes and comes looking…'

'And finds his mother in bed with his father,' Dev said smugly. 'He'd best get used to it.'

'Dev…'

'It's going to work, Maggie.' He hadn't heard the note of uncertainty enter her voice. He pulled her to him again, and kissed her long and deep—and the uncertainty in her mind faded to the point where it almost didn't exist.

Almost.

'I do need to go,' he said at last. He kissed her one last time and then hauled himself up from the bed—then stood looking down at her, drinking in the sight of her loveliness. 'Maggie…'

'Mmm?' She had to move, too, but she was sated…

'Organise yourself a life while I'm gone,' he said softly, looking down at her. 'Think about how you could be happy here, long-term. If you want to go back to nursing, then talk to the director of the local hospital. See if there are any part-time jobs. There'll be time enough when Dom goes to school. Buy yourself some clothes that don't scream Michael…'

'Dev…'

'Just think about the future,' he said softly, looking down at her with desire still blazing from his eyes. 'Our future. Because that's all I can think about. The future…and you.'

CHAPTER NINE

THE future was now.

Maggie had barely showered and dressed before Dominic woke. He staggered into her room, rubbing sleep from his eyes, and he grinned at her.

'Your hair looks like it had a tornado in the night.'

'Mmm.' Maggie checked it out. Dev had played with it in the night and that was what it looked like. She lifted her hairbrush and started brushing, shoving down an odd reluctance to leave it just as it was. To stay just as she was…

'Dad's about to leave,' Dom said. 'You want to come out and say goodbye?'

No. That was the last thing she wanted—to say goodbye—but somehow she made herself take Dom's hand, and together they went out to the verandah to watch Dev throw his gear in the car.

'You look after Maggie,' Dev told his son as he came up the verandah steps to greet them. 'Don't let her get into any trouble.'

'You'll be back Friday?' Dom said, trying hard not to sound anxious, and Dev lifted his son into his arms and hugged.

'I will. I promise. I have you and Maggie waiting for me. What better reason could a man have for coming home?' Then, without releasing Dom, he enveloped Maggie in his arms so Dom was squeezed between them in a bear hug.

For some stupid reason it was all Maggie could do not to cry.

'Hey…' He sensed her mood and pulled back. 'Maggie, what is it?'

'I…nothing.'

'I'll be back Friday. We'll go to the island Saturday.'

'We're still going to the island?' She kept the tremor from her voice, but only with a massive effort.

'I said we would,' he told her. 'We need to check on the aunts, see how it's all working—and then make decisions. But…I think some decisions have already been made—don't you?'

'I don't know.'

That stopped him. The smile died from his face. 'Maggie…'

But Mrs Collins was bustling from the front door. 'Mr Macafferty, that was your company secretary on the phone. He says he's at the airport already and where the hell are you?' She coughed and grinned at the words. 'Well, that's what he said.'

Dev swore, and looked at his watch. 'I still have twenty minutes. What's he fussing about?' Then he looked again at Maggie, and sighed as he saw the uncertainty on her face. 'Maggie, I have to go.'

'I know.'

'I'll be back.'

'I know that, too.'

There was no choice—but Dev slid into the car and left the farm knowing everything wasn't perfect.

The thought of her clouded face stayed with him on the drive to the airport. He flew to Sydney to catch the connecting overseas flight still thinking about it, and when the announcement came that there was a two-hour delay before the flight to New York he could no longer do nothing. This was too important.

So…what the hell could he do to make her feel welcome? As if she needed to stay.

She longed for independence, he knew. Sitting at home playing nursemaid to Dominic and wife to him would chafe her unbearably. Part-time nursing had to be the answer. Get her busy. Show her the community needed her as well as he and Dominic.

He'd told her to contact the hospital, but if there were no jobs…

Maybe he could do something there. He frowned. Who did he know on the board?

Three phone calls later the thing was done.

Great.

What else?

Dress shops. He wished he could go with her. Hell, if they didn't make her feel welcome…part of the community…

He'd given Mrs Collins a list to give her, but maybe it wasn't enough. If they pushed her to buy clothes she didn't want…

Maybe he shouldn't interfere…

'…regrets to announce a further delay to Flight 945…'

Well, that was fate. The address book was in his hand and the mobile phone was to hand.

He'd ring. It couldn't hurt to let them know she was special. Tell them to treat her as special…

It was just as well the plane was only two hours late—otherwise he would have rung every shop in Hobart!

So what was eating her?

Back at the farm, Maggie had taken Dom yabbying for the morning, but her sense of dreariness increased by the minute. What on earth was wrong? She should be the happiest woman in the world. She had everything.

She didn't. She didn't have her yearned for independence. More and more she was feeling it.

She was living on Devlin.

'Maggie, I reckon this yabby's the same one I caught yesterday.'

'Let's tag them properly,' she said, managing a grin 'Maybe we can get some waterproof paint and put numbers on their backs. By the time your dad gets home we could have Yabbies One to Two Thousand…'

A life of yabby numbering yawned before her. Good grief…

So… Do what Dev said, she told herself firmly. Think about a future. Get yourself a job.

Now. Do it now, before you talk yourself into trouble Before you talk yourself out of this life…

Making the appointment to see the director of nursing at the local hospital was amazingly easy. For some reason they almost seemed as if they were expecting her call— they were so welcoming.

Maybe they're short of nursing staff, she thought, and the idea cheered her. Nursing… She loved it. Michael had hated her working, and she'd only managed it part-time for the last few years, but it had been her only independence.

So it might still be.

She needed something to wear for the interview, so she left Dominic in Mrs Collins' cheerful care and took herself to Hobart.

Armed.

'This is the list of places Mr Macafferty said to use,' Mrs Collins told her. 'He said if you went shopping I was to tell you.'

Maggie looked at the list, and somehow her dark mood deepened.

She was being stupid, she told herself crossly. It was stupid to be annoyed by a list. Dev knew Hobart and she didn't. It wouldn't hurt to try…

'You must be Maggie.' She was no sooner through the door of the first boutique when the owner took right over from the junior sales assistant who'd first approached her. 'Dev told us you might be in. Welcome to Hobart, my dear. I recognised you from Dev's description. He said we were to show you the very best, and charge everything to him.…'

Oh, help…

Maggie backed out of the shop as if she'd been shot.

She tried two other shops and got exactly the same treatment. Angry now, she took herself to a chainstore, bought herself a cheap and nasty skirt she didn't want and then glared all the way back to the farm.

'You didn't buy very much, dear,' Mrs Collins said, eyeing her carrier bag with doubt and then eyeing Maggie's stormy face with more doubt.

'No. It was all organised for me, and I don't want to be organised.'

'What do you mean?'

'I mean he…Dev!…has rung around every decent place in town and organised me credit facilities so I don't have to worry my little head about money, and he's told the people in charge to look after me…and they all know he's as rich as can be, so do you think they'd show me anything of a reasonable price? You have to be kidding.'

'But…don't you like Mr Macafferty buying you clothes?' the older lady said, and Maggie's face grew thunderous.

'No, Mrs Collins, I do not!'

And then there was her interview with the director of nursing. The hospital looked wonderful. It was a tiny bush nursing hospital set in the hills out of Hobart, and Maggie felt her mood lift as she was ushered into the director's office.

Her happiness lasted a whole two seconds.

'We know all about you, my dear,' the woman said. 'Dev Macafferty rang my secretary and told her you'd probably be in. He arranged for us to receive references from your previous employer and he's given you a glowing reference himself. And he says you're settling permanently in the valley and would like part-time work. I can't tell you how delighted we are…'

It was all Maggie could do to stay civil. Somehow she got herself out of there and drove home, but every turn of the wheel deepened her sense of claustrophobia.

Didn't he see? Of all the moronic, overbearing, autocratic.…

She wanted her life! She didn't want to be a kept woman.

She might be head over heels in love with Devlin Macafferty—but she didn't want to be Dev's woman!

Four days wasn't long enough for a return trip to the US. He'd done it, but it had taken its toll. Dev drove home on Friday night as weary as he'd been in his life, but there was still the sense of tingling excitement at what lay ahead.

His son. And Maggie…

He hadn't been able to keep his mind from her the whole trip. He'd rung her a couple of times, but she wasn't good on the phone—polite but curt. Not the bubbly, vivacious Maggie he knew and loved.

Had she organised herself a job? he wondered. Ellen at the hospital had seemed sure they'd find a place for her. And clothes… She shouldn't have had any trouble there, and he was aching to see what she'd chosen.

He was aching to see her!

*   *   *

She wasn't aching to see him.

One look at her showed him that. Dev walked in the door and in seconds was surrounded by Dominic, dogs and noise. He lifted his son into his arms, hugged him hard, then looked over his head to Maggie and his smile died.

Maggie was smiling a welcome—sort of—but her face was so stiff and formal he knew the welcome was a lie.

'Hi,' she managed. 'Did you have a good trip?'

He took a step towards her through the tangle of yapping pups, but she backed off and shook her head.

'You must be hungry. We've waited dinner. I'll tell Mrs Collins you're here.' Her body language was giving him another message entirely.

'Maggie…'

'Tell us about your trip at dinner,' she said, and fled before he could say another word.

It was no better at dinner, though Dominic chatted cheerfully enough. He and Maggie had had a great time while he'd been away. Maggie had taken him to see the headmaster of the local school and Dom had spent an hour there already. The headmaster thought he could start next term— that was in four weeks—so he had a holiday until then. And he and Maggie were up to Yabby One Hundred and Two. Yabby Thirty-Four had been caught six times!

'That's great, Dom,' Dev said, but his eyes were still on Maggie.

'And we're still going back to the island tomorrow, aren't we?' Dom paused and cast a curious glance at Maggie, as if her silence was getting through. Then he looked at his father. 'I mean…you promised.'

Yeah. He'd promised. Not only had he promised Dominic, he'd promised Maggie. If she wanted an out, there it was, like it or not.

'The aunts seem to be getting on fine,' he said uneasily.

'We'll go back and spend the next few days with them, but the arrangements seem to be working out well.'

Wrong thing to say. Maggie's face closed as if it had shutters.

'For most of us,' she said.

'I don't…'

'I miss the island, Dev,' Maggie said quietly. 'I want to go back. For keeps.'

'Do you?'

'Yes.'

'You mean you might stay there for ever?' Dom asked, his small face creasing in perplexity. 'Why?'

'Because that's where I live.'

'But Grandpa said you were a…' Dom struggled to remember, and then his face cleared. 'A gift horse,' he said. 'You're a gift horse. That means you get to stay with us.'

'I'm not a gift horse, Dominic,' Maggie told him. She looked down at him, her eyes fixing his and willing him to understand. 'Dominic, I'm your friend. But I live on Listall Island. Not here. Any time you want to visit, then you'll always be very welcome, but your place is with your dad. And my place is with my grandpa.'

'You mean…Dad and I just have to visit?'

'If you want to see me,' Maggie said softly, 'then that's the way it has to be.'

'So are you going to tell me what's going on?'

It had taken ages to get the over-excited Dominic to bed. Dev had brought him a new computer game and there had been no way he was sleeping until he'd worked it out. Now, as Dominic finally settled, Maggie announced she was heading for bed, too. Her own bed.

'No way.' Dev moved in the hallway to block her path. 'Maggie, we need to talk.'

'I don't…'

'When I left,' Dev said carefully, 'I thought you were in love with me. You shared my bed. Now…it's as much as I can do to get you to speak to me.'

'I need to pack.'

'Not before you've told me what's going on.'

She closed her eyes. 'Dev, don't…'

'Tell me, Maggie.'

She paused, uncertainty and pain washing across her face. She was wearing her island clothes—jeans and an open-neck shirt. She mustn't have gone clothes shopping, Dev thought as he watched her face. She had her hair pulled back in that knot she wore—there wasn't a trace of make-up on her face—it was as if she was defiantly the old Maggie.

Apparently that was just what she was—or wanted to be.

'Devlin, I shouldn't have slept with you,' she said, in a voice that trembled. 'I was mad—a little bit crazy, I think. But…I don't want this. I've thought and thought while you've been away. I don't want to be the kept woman while you flit off around the world.'

His brow snapped down. 'That's hardly fair.'

'No, it's not,' she said evenly. 'I've had ten years of that. That's my share of hell, and I don't want any more.'

'Hell… If you're comparing me to Michael…'

'You're better at it than Michael,' she said. 'You don't manipulate as openly. But you manipulate just the same.'

'I don't manipulate.'

'Yes, you do,' she said evenly—so evenly that afterwards she would be proud of herself. All she felt like doing was crying, but somehow she managed to keep her face calm and herself on track. Away from the thought of what marriage to Dev could be… 'You organised me a job.'

'Maggie, I simply smoothed…'

'You organised me clothes. When I went to those bou-
tiques you listed, they knew already what I wanted—or
rather what you thought I wanted.'

'If you didn't like them...'

'Then I didn't have to buy them.' She was angry now,
and anger helped. He didn't see. 'But then you'd have been
hurt.'

'Hell, that's not true...'

'Maybe not, but I don't know that. I've no guarantees...and it's too big a chance to take.' She took a deep
breath and met his look with eyes that were unflinching.
'Dev, the clothes you organised...the job...they were great.
I was a fool to knock them back. But they weren't what
I'd organised. I've had a lifetime of being slotted into a
niche and I don't want it. For now, I want to be me.'

'You are you, Maggie,' he said carefully. 'If you don't
want what I organise then tell me—tell me to butt out.
Okay, I made a mistake, but that's no reason to shove me
out of your life. Tell me I'm an idiot and go from there.'

'How can I?'

He smiled then. 'Hey, it's easy. Say, "Devlin, you're a
fool." I do it to myself all the time.'

'Dev...' She faltered and her eyes searched his. Almost...

And then he stuffed it. 'Would it help if I said I loved
you?'

It didn't. Straight away he could see it didn't. Of all the
stupid... She'd actually flinched when he said the words.

Michael again?

'I don't think...' she said, and her voice had lost its calm.
'Dev, I don't think I know what that means. It's what Michael used to say whenever I threatened something he
didn't want me to. "But I love you..."'

'I've never said it before,' Dev said softly. 'I'm not Michael.' But even as he said it he knew it was useless. The words had acted as a trigger for her to run.

'Take me back to the island, Devlin,' she said wearily. 'I don't know what I'll do. If…if they're all happy there, then maybe I'll be totally free. Maybe I'll set off to make my fortune. But…for now…I want my freedom.'

'You don't want me?' Damn, his voice was forlorn. He felt like a pup who'd just been kicked…

'That's right,' she said with a tiny catch in her throat. 'I don't. I may be stupid, but I'm not yours, Dev. I belong to no one, and for now I don't need anyone. I don't need you.'

CHAPTER TEN

THEY flew to King Island and then took the supply boat to
Listall. Dominic, arms loaded with Wobble, seemed content, but he didn't understand Maggie's intentions.

'You mean, when we go home you won't come with us?'

'That's right. You have your dad and Mrs Collins and
Wobble.' She reached out and patted Wobble, who was
finding the sea trip not exactly to her liking. 'That's all you
need.'

Dom thought this over. 'I'll be lonely. My dad goes away
a lot.'

'Maybe he won't when I'm not there.'

Or…when he hasn't got his doormat, she added silently.
She cast a sideways look at Dev, who was standing in the
bow of the boat, facing the island ahead. His face looked
stern and forbidding. Dom followed her gaze and frowned
as well, a mirror image of his father.

'Dad wants you to stay with us.'

'He has you for company.' She rose and ruffled his hair.
'You and Wobble…what else could a man want?'

What else, indeed?

From where he stood, Dev could hear every word she
spoke, and he didn't like it one bit. He'd messed this right
up. He'd had the most wonderful chance in the world and
he'd blown it.

He'd come so close to succeeding…so near.

She was so beautiful… She was standing at the boat rail
as they approached Listall, the wind was in her hair and

the ocean was reflected in her eyes. There was a trace of sadness there that he so dearly wanted to remove…to kiss away the shadows…but he'd had his chance and he'd blown it. He'd moved too fast. Tried to make it so damned perfect.

And now… Every time he went near her, she put up her barriers and blocked him out. There was pain in her shuttered face, but that still didn't make it any less shuttered. He'd made her fearful, and he couldn't bear it.

And Dominic… It wasn't just he who'd miss Maggie like a part of him, he thought. He looked across at Dominic's now laughing face and he thought, My son's happiness is down to Maggie.

And he'd blown it!

What now? Give her time…?

Time. A breathing space. A year, maybe, to find out how lonely the world could be.

But she wouldn't be lonely, he thought savagely. If she went to the mainland and started nursing again…did he really think she'd be left alone a minute? Hell, no. She was too beautiful, and the men of the world weren't stupid.

Hell and hell and hell!

There was no more time for reflection. The boat was pulling in to the tiny island jetty and there were whoops from the headland above. Dev looked up as the aunts came hollering down the track towards them, followed by goats…

'Dev… Dominic… Maggie, dear… How lovely to see you.'

'Before we're enveloped…' Dev said suddenly—urgently—as the boat's motor died. 'Maggie?'

'Yes?' She looked at him, but the shutters—the barriers—still remained.

'Maggie, know that I love you,' he said softly—but loud

enough so he was sure she heard it. Dominic heard it too, and so did the boat captain. 'It has no strings. I'm not blackmailing. But, Maggie, whatever happens here…from now on… Know that even though I tackled this like a bull in a china shop, I did it because I'm head over heels in love with you. You've knocked me sideways. I want you, Maggie. I want you for my wife.'

'But I don't want to be your wife.'

There. As simple as that. So why was it tearing her heart out?

'Maggie…'

'I think…I think I love you, too, Dev,' she said steadily. 'That's the problem. I can't marry you and not be…your wife.'

'It doesn't make sense.'

'It does to me.'

'You could give it a try,' Dominic said anxiously, holding his puppy and staring at each of them in turn. 'Like me at boarding school.'

'We've tried it, Dominic,' Maggie said wearily. 'And it's like you trying boarding school—it isn't going to work.'

'Every single one of the goats has increased production. We're so proud of the girls. Even Ernestine… Did you know she wouldn't come near us for three days? Myrtle finally just wore her down…?'

'Wore her down?' Maggie said faintly. The aunts had taken her on a guided tour of their improvements and she was feeling stunned.

'We locked her in the dairy,' Molly said in satisfaction. 'It took both of us—and Lucy—half a day to get her in, and then Myrtle just sat. They glowered at each other for about four hours. Every time Ernestine glowered, Myrtle glowered harder, and every time Ernestine looked away,

Myrtle grabbed her ears and made her look at her again. Then she turned on the tape player and played jazz for another hour or two… Finally she hooked her up to the milking machine and Ernestine milked good as gold. Her supply's up with the best of them now.'

'I'll bet it is,' Maggie managed faintly. How could it not be? If she was Ernestine, she'd be pumping out milk, too. Pitting your will against the aunts was like swimming against the tide—ultimately impossible.

'So Myrtle and I think this venture is a success.' Molly eyed her sideways as she spoke. 'We'd love to stay on, and your grandpa's happy, too.'

He was. There was no denying that. The aunts were Joe's generation, and they had him fascinated. They'd taken over his life, but in the week she'd been away Joe had managed to improve his walking to the point where he could reach the beach and back. He was almost glowing.

'But Dev says…' Molly hesitated, and her eyes were suddenly, uncharacteristically uncertain. There was no mistaking the anxiety in the old lady's voice and Maggie flinched. 'Dev says you want to come back here.'

'You and Myrtle…would you really like to stay?'

'It's just what we've been dreaming of,' Molly breathed. 'We needed something…a challenge in our retirement, if you know what I mean, and we can't think of anything else we'd rather do. But if you and Dev aren't pairing off…'

'Dev and I have nothing to do with it,' Maggie said firmly.

'You and Myrtle and Grandpa are happy.'

'We're not putting you out of your home?'

'Molly, I don't think I want to spend the rest of my life here,' Maggie said honestly. 'If you'll stay here with Grandpa, then I'll go to the mainland and live.'

'Without Dev?'

'Without Dev.'

'Oh, my dear... We so hoped you'd marry.'

'I don't see why.'

'Joe says you need to be married.'

'That's chauvinistic nonsense,' Maggie said bluntly. 'You and Myrtle never married, and you've been happy.'

'But...we've never looked at a man like you look at Dev,' Molly told her. 'Oh, my dear, be very sure before you throw that away...'

Be very sure...

How on earth could she be that? Maggie spent the next two days trying very hard to be very sure—and at the same time avoiding Dev like the plague. He'd organised a helicopter pick-up on Tuesday, so he could get back to his precious general meeting, but meanwhile... If he went into a room, then she went out. The cottage was crammed with so many people, and Maggie took to being elsewhere as much as she could.

Dev noticed—of course he noticed—but for the most part he let her be, hoping that giving her space might work. Nothing else seemed to. She was so tight wired she sounded as if she'd snap any minute, and he had the sense to know her tension was down to him.

But he had to try. On Monday night—Dev's last night on the island—he could bear it no longer. He went searching and found her just where he'd expected, up on the outer platform of the lighthouse, staring bleakly out to sea.

'Communing with your boogies?'

She jumped as his hand fell on her shoulder, and she almost yelped.

'Do you mind?' she stuttered, pulling away as if she was burned. 'I could have fallen...'

'I would have held you,' he said evenly. 'There's no way I'd let you fall. Penny for them…'

'Penny?'

'For your thoughts.'

She stared blindly up at him—and then away, out to sea. 'I…I was just thinking it's coming up to a storm,' she managed lamely. 'The wind's getting up.'

'Liar.'

'It is. I don't know what else you…'

'You weren't thinking of the wind.'

'I was. You'll be lucky if your helicopter can land tomorrow if it gets any stronger.'

'Meaning you'll be stuck with me for another day.'

'I can stand it.'

'Another day of staying out of doors, trying to be where I'm not. That'll be hard if there's a storm.'

'Dev…'

'Maggie, don't do this.' He put his hands on her shoulders and drew her around to face him, gently drawing her in. He tilted her chin and looked down into those huge green eyes…a man could drown in those eyes… 'Maggie, you're tearing us in two.'

'We are two, Devlin,' she said steadily. 'Me and you. Two people with their own lives to lead.'

'No.' He shook his head as he gazed down at her. The feeling that had been building in him for the past weeks was becoming almost irresistible. Here was his heart. Here was the half of his whole. And to leave her would tear him apart. 'Maggie, all I want is you.'

'Yeah…' There was no mistaking the bitterness in her voice, and Dev swore as she pulled away from him again. Hell, he didn't have a clue what he was fighting here. The ghost of Michael? The ghost of ownership?

'Maggie, this goes both ways. Sharing our lives, I mean.

If you want to choose my clothes, then that's okay with me. If you want to organise me a job…run my life…'

'You know very well that it wouldn't be okay,' she snapped. 'You know you'd hate it.'

He grinned, abashed. 'Yeah, all right, I'd hate it. Like you hated it. But I've admitted it. I was stupid, insensitive, dopey…a great, blithering idiot. I'm like a big Labrador puppy, all excited because I've fallen in love. I just want you to have the best, Maggie.'

'But you still want me to fit into your life. Look after your son. Fit around the edges and be there for you when you get home…'

'I'll take you on whatever terms you care to name,' he said honestly. 'Maggie, I'll take you for half an hour a week if needs be. I'll organise the business so I stay home more. I was stupid to go to New York. I have managers…it's just realising I can delegate…'

'You love your business…your travel.'

'Not as much as I love you.'

Silence. The wind was rising by the minute. It was warm and sultry, the wind blowing strongly from the north with the promise of storms to come. It whipped Maggie's curls around her face in a cloud and Dev couldn't make out her eyes in the dimness. He couldn't guess what she was thinking.

He tried to take her hands, but she pulled away.

'Maggie, let's try…'

'We already did.'

'Just for a week…'

'No.' She lifted her hand to the moonlight, and her wedding ring was still on her finger. She stared at it for a long, long moment, then, in sudden decision, she wrenched it free and flung it out into the wind—out into the whirling whitecaps on the sea below. The tiny sob she gave as she flung it away was barely audible—but Dev heard it.

'There...' she said softly. 'I'm free. I'm free, Devlin. I belong to no man.'

'You can still love me,' he said softly, 'without becoming my possession. You'd never be that, Maggie.'

'You wouldn't know how to stop yourself,' she told him. She tilted her chin and met his look with defiance. 'You said yourself...you were stupid. That stupidity has cost me the chance of getting an impartial interview at your hospital. It's cost me the chance of choosing clothes without prejudice in the city. It's cost...'

'It's made people aware that I love you,' Dev said steadily. 'That's all, Maggie. Okay, I shouted my love from the rooftops, and it was way too soon and way too insensitive. But it doesn't mean there's nothing between us. I won't believe that, Maggie.'

'You'd better,' she said softly. 'Because that's the way it has to be. There's nothing.' She held up her ringless finger. 'Nothing. I'm on my own, Devlin, and that's just how I want to be.'

Dev lay awake for most of the night, while the wind steadily rose around the island. The storm was going to be a ripper. It suited his mood exactly, he thought bleakly. A howling gale was just what he felt like. Howling...

Bloody hell, this was impossible. To have met the perfect woman and to have rushed her...

She wouldn't come near him now. He knew that. She'd pushed past him and left him at the top of the lighthouse, and then, when he'd come in, she'd gone to bed and locked her bedroom door.

So that was that. If the storm permitted, then he'd take his son back to the mainland tomorrow and he and Dom would try and sort out a life without her. Heaven knew what Maggie would do. Make her own life? Whatever it was, she'd made it absolutely clear that whatever she did from now on she wanted nothing to do with him at all.

Hell!

You're a fool, Macafferty, he told himself over and over into the night, and the thought of Dom, who lay in the smaller bed beside him, just made it all worse. Dom could have loved her too—and she would have loved Dom—if he'd played his cards right.

'I'm sorry, Dom,' he whispered into the darkness against the sound of the howling wind. 'But I meant what I said to Maggie. I'll give up some of the business. I'll be home for you...'

Home without Maggie...

Hell!

He finally slept just before dawn, when the wind was reaching a crescendo. His last conscious thought was that the storm must be at its peak—but it wasn't.

He woke to banging. For a moment he thought it was banging on the door, but then he realised it was roofing iron, lifting and crashing down, lifting and crashing down...

Surely this was no normal storm... The sound was terrific!

He'd just flung back the bedcovers when the door opened and Joe walked in. He was dressed in his khaki fisherman's overalls as he leaned on his walking frame, and his face was urgent in the light of the lantern he'd lit in the passage...

'Storm's growing,' he said urgently as Dev reached his side. 'Been getting worse all night, and they reckon it's one out of the box. We've weathered some storms before, but this is as bad as it ever gets. Maggie's just been on the

radio to the mainland and they say the worst is to come.
They say a force ten gale's expected, or worse…'

'Force ten…'

'Fifty to sixty knots,' the old man said tersely. 'Thirty-
foot seas. Don't get much worse than that, and I've never
seen it that bad here. Structural damage, they're saying.
Trees uprooted, that sort of thing. The island don't have
much in the way of trees, but the house… I reckon this
house is shot, boy. Wake 'em up. I might be fussing, but I
want everyone in the lighthouse…'

'But…' Dev thought fast. 'Thirty-foot seas…the lighthouse…'

'Lighthouse is built to take that and worse,' the old man
said. 'The house isn't. It's too old to take it. The iron's
lifting off the roof already. You can hear. We need to get
out. I'm shoving a few things together. Water bottles. Bit
of food. But there's not much time. You wake the aunts
up, and the boy, and move them to the lighthouse. Fast.'

And he turned and stumped off down the passage with
a speed that would have made Maggie proud.

Maggie…

There was no time to think of Maggie. Dev had an urgent
job to do, and he did it.

Fifteen minutes later he had the aunts, Dominic and
Wobble, blanketed, warm and secure within the vast lighthouse walls. He hadn't had time to think. He'd just moved.
The aunts, normally efficient, practical and totally dependable, had shown their age when he'd woken them. They
were in a strange place, and the wind was terrifying. Their
confusion showed, slowing him. Amazingly, it was Dominic who was calm.

'We'll be okay,' he told his father as he settled them in
the light chamber. 'Maggie told me this lighthouse is built

to last for a thousand years. You go back and get Maggie and Grandpa.'

Dev blessed him—and went. Maggie and Joe must both be packing belongings, he thought, but there was no more time for packing. He emerged from the lighthouse and the wind hit him like a physical blow. Packing was no longer a priority.

Life was.

The sheets of iron were lifting from the house as he emerged in the pre-dawn light, the sheets being hurled southward, away from the lighthouse. The wind was reaching a speed where it was almost impossible to walk against it.

The house was south of the lighthouse—so he was almost blown back. Get them out of there…

Joe was in the kitchen. A gaping hole had ripped out of the ceiling above his head, but still Joe worked on, shoving things into containers. He barely looked up as Dev entered—as though he'd been expecting him.

'We'll take that basket,' Joe said, raising his voice to be heard over the wind and pointing. 'And this one here.' Then, amazingly, he hauled forward his bath chair and plonked his elderly frame in it. 'I'll be more stable in this, boy,' he growled. 'I'll never get to the lighthouse on the frame. Shove the baskets on me lap. I'll hang on and you push.'

There were three photograph albums on the seat underneath him, Dev noticed grimly. Joe wasn't saying…but to have to leave everything, knowing it would be destroyed…

But Maggie… Where was she?

'Joe, where's Maggie?' he said urgently. 'Is she still packing? She has to get out of here.'

'She went to get the goats. She ought to be back by now.'

She said to get everyone to the lighthouse and she'd meet us there.'

'The goats…?'

'You heard.' Another sheet of iron crashed away from the house and the old man winced. 'Move, boy. I don't want to be in this lot when it comes down.'

'But Maggie…'

'She'll be back. I told you, she'll have gone straight to the lighthouse.'

'She's not there yet.'

The old man's face twisted in fear. 'But…she said…' He rose, but Dev pushed him back in the chair.

'Tell me.'

'She's taken Lucy…she said she'd lock the goats in the dairy and get back to the lighthouse.'

'When did she go?'

'Half an hour ago,' Joe managed. 'Hell, boy…'

'Let's get you to the lighthouse,' Dev said grimly. 'And then, if she's still not back, I'll go and find her.'

The dairy was hopeless.

It had been built much later than the house, and it was stronger, but not strong enough. By the time Maggie reached it and found the goats sheltering in the lee of its walls she knew already what she must do.

Maybe if the wind was now at its worst then the dairy would hold—but maybe not. And if it didn't…if the wall protecting them crumbled away… then she held no hope at all for her thirty-strong herd.

Where else? She'd thought they'd be safe in the dairy, but it was growing increasingly obvious that they wouldn't be. She couldn't wedge them all into the lighthouse, and to go to the lighthouse would be to fight northwards, into the wind!

Ernestine came to meet her, nosing forward, her ears flattened and her flanks quivering. Her fear was palpable.

Thank heaven they weren't sheep, Maggie thought grimly. Goats had personalities. They trusted her. With luck they'd follow...

The cave! It was their only hope!

'Ernestine, we have to go to the cave,' she told the goat, and watched her goaty face for reaction. Stress could kill a goat so fast... She put her hands around her neck and hugged. 'Help me, Ernestine.' She didn't really expect the goat to understand, but she desperately needed her trust—and to talk to anything was a relief. Maggie had never felt such a wind in her life! 'If you go, the herd'll follow,' she told her. 'If I get you to the cave then we'll be safe.'

They had so little time. There was sand whipping up from the beach, slashing across the island like a thousand razors. If they didn't move now...

The cave was to the south, so the wind would be behind them. That meant at least the goats' eyes would be protected, and they were like dogs. They'd learned that people could mean security. They could trust...

All right... The only thing to do here was to try.

'Way back, Lucy,' she told the dog. 'Bring 'em up. Way back...'

The dog stared at her as if she was mad, but Maggie was already holding Ernestine by the ears and bringing her forward, out of the shelter of the wall. Who knew if the wall would keep standing? It was a chance Maggie wouldn't take.

'Let's go. Way back...' And with Ernestine at her side, her hand clutching a handful of goat hair in case Ernestine had other ideas, she started running.

Lucy scooted around the back of the herd and gave a

few nudges forward. The goats stared out at their leader in astonishment.

Lucy nudged some more—and then Maggie, Lucy and thirty goats were running across the wind-battered island as if their lives depended on it.

It took ten minutes of running to reach the cave, and by the time they arrived the wind was screaming and the sea was a mass of slashing white foam. If the cave had been on the north of the island it would have been full of water, driven in by the wind. As it was, with the cave in the lee of the island, they hit the beach, entered the dark recesses of the cavern, and peace hit them like a blanket.

The reaction was almost overwhelming.

'Oh, Lucy… Oh, Ernestine…' Maggie sank down on the floor of the cave and put her arms around dog and goat. Her whole body was stinging. She was wearing jeans and a windcheater, but no socks with her sneakers. Now her ankles were bleeding from the stinging sand. Her neck was the same, grazed raw, and a branch had hurled itself at her somewhere on the run and smashed into her legs.

How many goats…? She hadn't looked behind as she'd run. If she had, she would have been blinded by the sand. She'd been aware of goats around her—most of the herd must have followed—but…

She caught herself and rose, making a swift head-count. Twenty-eight…

Two missing.

Should she go back for them?

She walked back to the cave entrance and looked out. That shot that idea. There was no way… The sand would be a stinging wave across her head. To face that…

A sheet of galvanised iron hurled cross the headland

above her head, smashed onto the rocks at the cave entrance and then bumped out to sea.

Iron… The house.…

They'd all be in the lighthouse by now, she told herself. They'd be safe.

Thank God she'd come when she had. Thank God she'd had this warning…

It was only because she hadn't been able to sleep that she'd risen and listened to the weather report. The island was accustomed to storms, but this one… With no warning they would have lost all the goats. Once the iron had started ripping from the house then they would have made it to the lighthouse for safety, but to lose Ernestine and the girls…

They'd lost two… Maggie looked out at the smashing rubble flying out to sea and she held no hope at all for the missing goats. A lump as big as an apple rose in her throat, threatening to choke her. Damn…

At least the people were safe, she told herself fiercely. Joe and the aunts and Dom…

And Dev…

Crazy that it was so important…

Crazy that she wanted Dev. She wanted Dev right now!

At least he was safe…

But Dev wasn't safe at all.

'Maggie…'

It was stupid to shout. His voice was being carried away on the wind, and there was no way she'd hear. But with every step he managed towards the dairy, the fear in his heart grew greater. The dairy wouldn't stand in this. She should be coming back.

Where the hell was she?

But…the dairy was still standing. He could see it though

the stinging sand. She must still be in there, with her dratted goats.

'Maggie!'

He reached the door, which was already hanging askew, blasted from its hinges.

'Maggie!'

Nothing. Nothing!

With a heart icy with fear he made his way though to the inner room. The windows had smashed and the place was filling with sand. The noise was deafening. Where…?

With a massive, creaking, shattering groan, the whole roof lifted upward. The wall beside him buckled and the timbers smashed sideways. Dev put his hands upward to stop the mass of timber crashing down…

Nothing more.

CHAPTER ELEVEN

THE storm raged for almost five hours, and when it was over Maggie emerged to a world she hardly recognised. The island was windswept and barren at the best of times, but now... It looked washed, she thought bleakly. It was as if a massive tidal wave had covered the island, sweeping all before it, and all that was left was sand...

It wouldn't destroy it. She hauled herself up onto the bluff, and her feet touched turf through the thick layer of sand. After the first rain, the tough island grasses would break through again. The goats would find enough to survive.

The island would go on...

But...her home...

She could see the lighthouse from where she stood, its solidity giving her a first taste of reassurance. That was where they'd be, she thought. Her people. Dev...

The wind was slackening dramatically. Any minute they'd emerge to see the damage.

But the house...

The house was gone. She should be able to see the roof from here, but there was no roof...

What about the dairy?

No. She shaded her eyes. Nothing. There was no roofline behind the sandhills...

Thank heaven she'd taken the goats to the cave.

She stood, silently looking at the damage, while Lucy stood pressed by her side and twenty-eight goats assembled behind her in goat-like awe. Even they were stunned to

178

silence, their natural curiosity stilled. Two of their number were gone…

Then Ernestine put her nose down and foraged under the sand to find the turf.

And the rest of them followed her lead. Life returning…

'I need to find your friends,' Maggie said sadly, knowing it'd be a bleak task. Two missing goats…

But then she paused at a shout from the direction of the dairy. She shaded her eyes again, and saw the two old ladies practically racing towards her. They were waving wildly, and their relief was palpable even from a distance.

'Maggie… Oh, Maggie, my dear…'

Aunt Myrtle reached her first, wrapping her arms around her and bursting into tears. 'Oh, Maggie, we were so worried. When we saw the dairy…'

'It's just a pile of splintered timber,' Molly gulped behind her. 'When we saw it we were so frightened. Then Myrtle found a dead goat. But then she said…if you'd all been in there, then there would have been thirty dead goats. It would have been obvious, and we could only find two, and they were both outside…'

'So we knew…or we hoped we knew…that you'd found somewhere else to take cover. Oh, my dear, and you had. And all your precious goats…'

'We're fine,' Maggie said quickly, hugging each of them in turn. 'And you? You're all okay? Dev and Dom and Grandpa are fine?'

Molly hauled herself out of her arms and stared. 'Dev?'

'He's okay?' Maggie demanded, her heart quickening in fear.

'Oh, my dear, Joe and Dom are fine. But Devlin… My dear, isn't he with you?'

Three minutes later, they found him in the dairy—or what was left of the dairy. One of the massive refrigerators had fallen, locking him between that and what was left of the wall.

He lay absolutely still where he'd fallen, and his face was deathly pale. For one awful, heart-stopping moment, Maggie thought he was dead—and in that moment her life changed for ever.

CHAPTER TWELVE

DEV woke to Maggie.

He felt her before he opened his eyes. There were fingers gripping his hand, and he'd know that touch anywhere. For a moment he lay still, savouring the moment, half afraid if he opened his eyes he might be proved wrong.

'Dev…?'

Her voice… His eyes flickered open, wincing at the light, but she was there and it was worth the pain. She was Maggie as he'd never seen her before—windswept, her hair a tangled mess, bloodstains on her face and neck and her dusty face stained with tears, but she was gazing at him with a look in her eyes that made his heart almost stop.

'Maggie…' His voice came out a croak and she gave a long, joyful laugh, buried her face in his chest and burst into tears.

'Oh, damn you… You rat, you had me so worried. If you knew how terrified I've been…' Her tangled curls were tumbled across his chest, and her voice was muffled by bedclothes.

Bedclothes…

He put his hand in her hair and let his fingers drift as his eyes took in his surroundings. Lights… White…

He was in hospital!

'Maggie, what have you done to me?' he asked slowly, and she raised her head and managed a watery smile. 'Where am I?'

'You're in Melbourne. Don't you remember the helicopter bringing you here?'

No. Or maybe he did... He vaguely remembered pain, and voices, and more pain. And Maggie leaning over him and telling him not to worry, she'd given him...

No. It was all just a blur.

'You've banged your head again,' she told him. 'And guess what? I managed to get it photographed this time.'

'Yeah?'

'Yeah.' She gripped both his hands and held hard. 'Nothing to see, though. You lost consciousness, but you've a thick skull.'

'Have I?' He was sounding inane, but it was hard to make any sense from the fog. It was hard to make himself think at all.

'You've broken your leg, Dev,' she told him gently. 'They gave you an anaesthetic to set it. That's why you're feeling so dopey.'

'So I'll live?'

'You'll live.'

Silence. He closed his eyes again and Maggie thought he'd drifted back to sleep—but his hand moved to grip hers.

'You're real?'

'I'm real.'

'I thought you were dead,' he whispered, and the fear he'd felt was still real and terrible. It drifted around the room, and Maggie's fingers held his as hard as his held hers.

'Well, ditto,' she said unsteadily. 'And I had more reason. You go around lying unconscious under wrecked buildings...'

'Where were you?'

'In the cave. Safe as houses. Or rather safe as caves.'

'I might have known,' he managed, and his grip on her tightened. 'A pirate's treasure cave. Treasure...'

'Dev...'

'Stay,' he said wearily, and his eyes drifted closed. There was no way he could keep them open longer. 'Please.'

For answer, she leaned across and kissed him very softly on the lips, and her words might almost have been part of his dreaming.

'I'll stay,' she said softly. 'This is my place. With you.'

When he woke again she was yellow.

Dev blinked, and blinked again, but he wasn't dreaming. This was a very different Maggie...

She'd showered and changed. Her hair gleamed, brushed and clean, but still a mass of riotous curls. The curls he loved... Her face was no longer dust and tear-stained, and there was no trace of blood on her skin. The few shallow scratches had been washed...

But her clothes...

She was wearing some sort of skirt, as long as her home-spun, but it wasn't homespun. It was cotton, he thought dazedly, brilliant yellow cotton, with flounces of a deeper gold...

And a blouse, tight-fitting, cut low across her breasts, with the same gold filigree threaded through the edging...

Good grief!

'What on earth...?'

'You like my skirt?' she said, and grinned—and rose to pirouette as she'd done on that first night on the island.

'I love your skirt,' he told her.

'So do I. I had to get back before you woke up, so my shopping time was limited, but I managed a heap. It's easy when you have money.'

'Yeah?' He thought this through. 'You have money?'

'Mmm.'

His head wasn't working right. 'I thought you were broke.'

'No. I was stupid.' She smiled, and her smile was like a sunbeam. Pure happiness. 'Michael hated me working and he wouldn't let me touch my money. When he died I gave all his money to charity, but I didn't touch mine. I knew I was being stupid, giving it away, but spending it was like…going against Michael one last time.'

'And now you feel free to spend it?' He was struggling to understand here, but it was starting to feel good.

'Yes,' she said softly She smiled at him and sat down to take his hand. 'Because that's exactly what I am. Free.'

'I see.' He didn't. There was still fog. He was fighting to focus on anything more than her smile. 'You mean… you're free to do anything you like.'

'Yes,' she told him, and her smile widened and there was love in her voice. 'I'm free to be me. I'm free to do whatever I want with my life. And…'

'And?' Dear God, he hardly dared hope.

'And I'm free to love you,' she told him softly. 'I'm free to do what I like, and that's what I want. I want to wear yellow clothes. I want to leave my hair free. I want to love Dominic and Grandpa and Molly and Myrtle and Lucy and Wobble and all my crazy goats…but most of all I want to love you, Devlin Macafferty.'

'Love me?'

'Love you.'

Hell! He was trussed up like a Christmas turkey and she was smiling at him from the other side of the room. He couldn't move and he was being granted the most precious thing in the world. More precious than life itself.

All he wanted to do now was gather her in his arms. To take her to him and never let her go. And all he could do was stare at her with dazed, uncomprehending eyes and open and shut his mouth like a goldfish!

'That doesn't mean I'm taking you on your terms,' she

said sternly, trying to suppress her smile and stepping back even further from the bed.

'No?'

'No. So don't look at me like that—like you're some hopeful Labrador puppy.'

'No, ma'am.' For the life of him he couldn't think of a more intelligent thing to say.

'You can tell me if you like my clothes or not, but if I disagree then I can tell you to go jump. And vice versa.'

'Yes, ma'am.'

'I can work if I want.'

'Of course.'

'If you travel, then I can travel.'

'You think I'll travel? If you're home? A man would be mad.'

'Shut up,' she told him kindly. 'I haven't finished yet.'

'No ma'am.'

'I like you docile,' she told him, grinning. 'I think I'll keep you trussed.'

'Bondage, huh? Maggie come here.'

'Not before...' Her face clouded. 'Not before I say something else.'

'What?' Something bad. He could see it on her face.

'I want to say I'm sorry, Dev,' she said softly. 'For not taking you on trust. For not loving you. When I saw you...when I thought you were dead... Dev, I saw that I'd been offered something so precious and I'd nearly lost it. Dev, I'm so sorry...'

'Is that all?' His face cleared. 'Maggie, see this contraption?' He gestured to the elaborate set of wires and pulleys over the bed.

'Yes.'

'If you're not here in two seconds then I'm pulling them off and coming to fetch you.'

'But…'

'No more buts.'

'Dev…'

'Come here and be kissed senseless, woman,' he growled. 'Before I go completely around the twist. And you wouldn't want a husband who was around the twist, now, would you?'

'No…' She took one step forward.

'Faster,' he said, and leaned out of the bed towards her— so fast that she had to sweep forward and catch him before he fell…

There was no choice then.

He was already in her arms—and she was being kissed so senseless that she might never regain her senses again.

As weddings went…well, it was different.

It was small, for one thing. The only ones present were the vicar, two elderly women and one old man, one small boy, two dogs—a mature and puzzled Lucy with a half-grown Wobble—oh, and one goat, there in representative capacity. Ernestine was representing the herd.

The setting was the outer railings of Listall Island light-house. Right up at the top. It was twilight, with a soft moon rising on the horizon and it was the most beautiful setting in the world.

The setting was fitting. One man and one woman were making vows that would last a lifetime…

They'd been back on the island for two weeks now. It had taken two months to let a team of builders rebuild the place. There was still so much to do, but the billy goat had done his work. The girls of the herd were wearing identical smug expressions. Come spring, the island would be running with kids, and Windswept Cheeses would be in full production again.

They were all infinitely content. Dom hadn't touched his computer for weeks. The aunts were bossing to their hearts' content. Joe was beaming from ear to ear. Life was infinitely good for all of them…

Joe wasn't smiling as much as Dev. Dev looked down at his bride and there was no mistaking the pride and love in his eyes.

His Maggie…

His lovely Maggie.

And the bride?

The bride wore her heart in her eyes as well. Her Dev… Her lovely Dominic. All her family…

Some time tonight she'd tell him, she thought. Tell her love…that kid goats weren't the only babies due to be born in this vicinity in the near future…

This dress would soon no longer fit. But meanwhile…

Meanwhile, the bride wore a stunningly lovely yellow gown, a gown chosen by herself—with a little advice from Dominic, from Myrtle and Molly, from Joe and even from Devlin.

From her family—the people she'd chosen to trust with all her heart.

MILLS & BOON®

Makes any time special

Enjoy a romantic novel from
Mills & Boon®

Presents...™ *Enchanted*™ TEMPTATION.

Historical Romance™ MEDICAL ROMANCE™

COMING NEXT MONTH

MILLS & BOON®

Enchanted™

THE NINE-MONTH BRIDE by Judy Christenberry

Susannah longed for a baby and Lucas desperately wanted a son, but not the emotional ties of marriage. So they decided to make a convenient marriage, then make a baby - the old-fashioned way…

THE BOSS AND THE BEAUTY by Donna Clayton

Cindy was determined to make her boss, Kyle, see her as a woman rather than his employee. But as Kyle *never* mixed business with pleasure—it was going to be a long haul to get this man from the boardroom to the altar!

TAMING JASON by Lucy Gordon

Jason was injured and temporarily blind, and for his sake Elinor must keep her identity a secret. What would happen when he was able to see her again - and recognise her as the woman he'd once considered unsuitable for marriage?

A HUSBAND WORTH WAITING FOR by Grace Green

After his accident Jed's memory loss turned him into an entirely different man. Sarah found him charming—even seductive! But how long until Jed's memory returned? And when it did, would he still be a husband worth waiting for?

Available from 4th February 2000

*Available at most branches of WH Smith, Tesco, Martins,
Borders, Easons, Volume One/James Thin
and most good paperback bookshops*

COMING NEXT MONTH

MILLS & BOON®

Enchanted™

BORROWED BACHELOR by Barbara Hannay

Maddy needed a man who'd pretend to be her boyfriend, and her sexy neighbour Rick seemed ideal. Yet Rick played the part of the attentive lover so convincingly that even Maddy's mind turned towards marriage…

MEANT FOR YOU by Patricia Knoll

Jed thinks Caitlin is too uptight. She thinks Jed is too laid-back. All they have to do is stick to their separate sides of the house. So why do they keep meeting in the hallway?

MARRYING MARGOT by Barbara McMahon

The worst time in Rand's life had been when he and Margot had lost their baby and their young marriage had floundered. Now Rand wanted a reconciliation and more children. Margot still loved him, but she couldn't go through the heartache again…

THE BILLIONAIRE DADDY by Renee Roszel

Baby Tina needed a mum and her aunt Lauren wanted to take on the role—as soon as she had dealt with Tina's so-called 'father', Dade Delacourt. When Dade mistook Lauren for Tina's nanny the mistake gave Lauren the ideal opportunity to check out Dade's parenting skills. Except the plan backfired because the irresistible billionaire expected her to be with him twenty-four hours a day…

Available from 4th February 2000

2 FREE

books and a surprise gift!

We would like to take this opportunity to thank you for reading this Mills & Boon® book by offering you the chance to take TWO more specially selected titles from the Enchanted™ series absolutely FREE! We're also making this offer to introduce you to the benefits of the Reader Service™—

★ FREE home delivery
★ FREE gifts and competitions
★ FREE monthly Newsletter
★ Exclusive Reader Service discounts
★ Books available before they're in the shops

Accepting these FREE books and gift places you under no obligation to buy, you may cancel at any time, even after receiving your free shipment. Simply complete your details below and return the entire page to the address below. *You don't even need a stamp!*

YES! Please send me 2 free Enchanted books and a surprise gift. I understand that unless you hear from me, I will receive 4 superb new titles every month for just £2.40 each, postage and packing free. I am under no obligation to purchase any books and may cancel my subscription at any time. The free books and gift will be mine to keep in any case.

N0EA

Ms/Mrs/Miss/Mr ....Initials.....................................
                                          BLOCK CAPITALS PLEASE

Surname ....

Address ....

....

....Postcode...................................

Send this whole page to:
UK: FREEPOST CN81, Croydon, CR9 3WZ
EIRE: PO Box 4546, Kilcock, County Kildare (stamp required)

Offer valid in UK and Eire only and not available to current Reader Service subscribers to this series. We reserve the right to refuse an application and applicants must be aged 18 years or over. Only one application per household. Terms and prices subject to change without notice. Offer expires 30th June 2000. As a result of this application, you may receive further offers from Harlequin Mills & Boon and other carefully selected companies. If you would prefer not to share in this opportunity please write to The Data Manager at the address above.

Mills & Boon is a registered trademark owned by Harlequin Mills & Boon Limited.
Enchanted is being used as a trademark.